AENTI SARAH'S CHRISTMAS

Amish Romance

❧

HANNAH MILLER

Tica House
Publishing

Sweet Romance that Delights and Enchants!

Personal Word from the Author

❦

To My Dear Readers,

How exciting that you have chosen one of my books to read. Thank you! I am proud to now be part of the team of writers at Tica House Publishing who work joyfully to bring you stories of hope, faith, courage, and love.

Please feel free to contact me as I love to hear from my readers. I would like to personally invite you to sign up for updates and to become part of our **Exclusive Reader Club** —it's completely Free to join! Hope to see you there!

With love,

Hannah Miller

VISIT HERE to Join our Reader's Club and to Receive Tica House Updates:

https://amish.subscribemenow.com/

Contents

Chapter One

With tears streaming down her face, Sarah Fisher stared at the still smoldering ruins of the barn where her brother, Ivan, and his wife, Jennifer, had lost their lives.

Smoke still clogged the night sky, obscuring the stars.

The night was chilly, but the fire had warmed the air all around the barn.

How had it happened? They'd had a lantern to light the barn, but it wasn't near the hay. And the utmost care was always taken to prevent this exact thing. And yet, the barn had caught fire earlier in the night after they'd come home from visiting an elderly neighbor.

Ivan and Jennifer had turned the horse out into the back pasture but must have returned to the barn. Something had happened to that lantern. Still, why hadn't they had time to escape? It made no sense at all. She would never know what had caused the accident or why they had been trapped inside. But what would knowing help anyway?

How could they be gone? And to have died in such an unbearable way. Horrifying visions filled her head. Maybe they had died from the smoke instead of the flames. She couldn't bear the thought of the agony they had gone through.

She and the children had been in the house playing board games. They hadn't known anything was wrong. Because they'd been playing in the back sewing room, she hadn't even known her brother and sister-in-law had come home yet. She hadn't heard the buggy.

But they'd heard the sirens of an approaching fire engine. She'd thought nothing of it until the firetruck turned into the driveway and the noise was deafening. The three of them had raced to the side door, and that's when they saw the barn engulfed in flames so high, it must have been seen for miles.

And just like that, her entire world crashed down around her.

She rushed toward the barn only to be stopped by a fireman who wouldn't let her go near the blaze. When she saw the buggy had returned, she'd stood there screaming in anguish as the barn caved in. The fireman had led her away and left her and the children in the care of an elderly neighbor.

Thank God the neighbors had taken her eleven-year-old nephew and nine-year-old niece to their home. She had waited to see their parents' bodies removed from charred rubble, and it had almost been more than she could take. Thank God the children weren't there to see something so horrible they would never forget.

All she could think about, over and over, was that she was alone, at seventeen, to care for the children and keep them safe. She was utterly stunned but determined not to let anyone see it. She had to be strong for Peter and Anna. She was all they had left.

Why had her brother and his beautiful wife been snatched away so cruelly? Why had God called them home? She didn't understand. *Couldn't* understand. All she knew as she stood there in the aftermath of the huge fire, smelling the burnt, soggy wood, was that her entire world as she had known it was gone.

Now she had two children to raise and their parents' business to run to support the three of them. She didn't know how she was going to do it all by herself. But there was no one else. She would not let the children be split up. No matter how hard she had to work, she would keep them together—the three of them.

Sarah squared her shoulders and wiped away her tears. She said a prayer then turned and trudged to the house she'd called home since her own parents had died in a buggy accident on a lonely Rock Point highway years before.

Maybe she would wake up and find it was all an awful dream. She desperately wanted to believe that. But she wasn't sleeping, and it wasn't a dream. She went inside to the kitchen and sat at the table. She glanced at the wall clock. How was it nearly three in the morning already? Unable to stop them, tears rolled silently down her cheeks.

She'd shared so many meals at this table with fellowship, laughter, and joy. Now it was all gone. What was she going to say to Peter and Anna? How was she going to comfort them when her life was in complete wreckage, too?

She knew how hard it was going to be for them. She'd been there herself. She had so often thanked God for her brother, Adam. He and his wife, Jennifer, had taken her in, given her a home, and loved her. Now, silently, she vowed to do the same for their children.

She couldn't take their parents' place, and she didn't want to, but she would keep them together. She would give them the love they needed and always be there for them.

No matter what.

~

Three days following the fire, Sarah managed to appear calm and as serene as possible, though inside she was falling apart.

She didn't want to look at the two closed, simple pine caskets, but she couldn't take her eyes from them.

Thinking about her brother and Jennifer brought so much pain, it was almost more than she could bear.

Thomas Weaver, her fiancé, stood quietly next to her. At least she still had him in her life. No matter how bad things were, and they were as bad as they could get, he would be there for support.

People greeted her, gave condolences, and assured her and the children that their loved ones were in the arms of God—but the entire day took place in a fog. It had been much the same when her own parents had gone home to the Lord.

As she stood there with the children beside her, all she could think was that her brother and Jennifer were inside those boxes. She couldn't even concentrate as the bishop began the service with prayer.

Her brother and sister-in-law had been there for her and had picked up the pieces when she lost her mother and father. And now, she found herself in the same position, but without the confidence of having more years and experience to guide her.

Never in her seventeen years had the future seemed so frightening and impossible. Never had she been so alone with such responsibility on her shoulders. And yet, she had no choice but to carry on and be the rock the children needed.

She glanced at Thomas. Of course, she wasn't truly alone, but it was her responsibility until she and Thomas were married. And that was more than a year away.

Thomas stared straight ahead, seemingly lost in thought.

The room was packed with friends and others from the community who'd come to pay their respects. Many had offered words meant to comfort, but they'd barely registered through her loss and the mountain of worries gnawing at her mind.

Her best friend, Rebecca Troyer, stood close by with her family. She could count on Rebecca, too. They'd been best friends since they were six years old.

The house smelled of the food staying warm on the stove and in the oven for the attendees who would gather after the burial. Though she wouldn't be able to eat more than a bite or two, she'd helped prepare the food as was customary for those who would want to share a meal.

A couple of the older women had taken over the kitchen so she could attend the services.

When they hymns began, she tried to sing, but her ears had a strange ringing, and she was having difficulty following along. After the hymns, the bishop began the sermon which went on for a good while.

Anna and Peter moved closer to her.

Her sorrow for them was bone deep. They were still in shock from the loss of their parents. And beneath her facade of calm, she was frightened for them as well as for herself. What was going to happen now? She'd vowed to keep them together. And she would. But she wasn't a fool. It was going to be anything but easy.

She pulled at her collar and just wanted the day to end. If only she could go curl up under one of the quilts she'd made and pretend none of it was happening—it was all just a bad dream she'd soon awaken from. How was it even possible that just four days ago everything had been good and right? How could her life and the children's lives be turned upside down in a matter of hours?

Now she had others relying on her, and her alone.

No matter how much Thomas might want to help, it fell on her to take care of the family business, the house, and the children. Thomas was a good man, but there was only so much time he could spend with her. He had his own business to run.

Anna grabbed Sarah's hand and held on tightly. Sarah slipped her arm around the little girl, trying to give what comfort she could.

She shook her head slightly, as if to clear the frightening thoughts away, then she lifted her chin. She was alone in responsibility, but she wasn't alone in life. Thomas was there. He would help her when he could. And Anna and Peter where there, and they needed her. And she would raise them the same as their father and mother had raised her.

After what seemed like an eternity, she bit the inside of her cheek to keep from bursting into tears as the bishop's sermon drew to a close. She knew what came next. It was almost time for the trip to the district's cemetery. Time to watch her beloved family lowered into the graves dug by men from the community.

Those same men would shovel the cold dirt back into the holes, completing the burial of her loved ones. And it would all be over and life would go on. Though it would never be the same again, it would go on.

All too soon, the caskets were carried out and put into a large wagon. Two beautiful black horses, meticulously clean and groomed, were hitched to it.

She led the children out to her brother's buggy and helped them in before she climbed up beside them. Thomas sat beside her. In a daze, she watched as Thomas picked up the reins, and they took their place behind the wagon while the other mourners lined up behind them.

It was time to go. She squeezed her eyes closed for a moment. Then the wagon rolled forward.

Chapter Two

The first week after the funeral, passed quickly for Sarah. Before the accident, she'd often walked the children to school, either by herself or with Jennifer, so that was already part of her routine. She usually did some of the outdoor barn chores, too.

She'd always done more than necessary, out of gratitude, to contribute to the household.

It wasn't that she didn't know how to do the work, she did. It was just overwhelming to be responsible for all of it.

The only thing she wasn't experienced with was running the woodshop. When it came to that, she was lost. Her brother had run it alone.

She glanced up at the rumble of buggy wheels. Thomas's liver chestnut trotted up the driveway.

It was only the second time she'd seen him since the funeral. Maybe she should have been annoyed with him, but she was so glad to see him that she couldn't quite manage annoyance —even if he did deserve it.

He pulled up his horse and jumped down. She hurried over to his buggy.

"Sarah, how are you?" His gaze traveled past her as if scanning for something out of order.

"I'm doing all right," she said. "I guess." Was she doing all right? Or was she still wandering around in a daze? Probably the latter.

"Have you got the woodworking shop going again?"

"*Nee.* The two workers are coming back soon," she said.

"*Gut.* You have to get money coming in so you can take care of things," he said.

"I know." She was well aware of her situation. "Would you like some *kaffe*? It's chilly this morning."

"That would be right nice."

"Come, let's go sit in the kitchen," she said.

"Sounds *gut*."

Thomas followed her inside the house through the back kitchen door.

"Make yourself at home," she said and set about putting the coffee on the stove. She got a couple of mugs, sugar and cream, and then joined him at the table.

"You haven't done the morning work yet, have you?" he said.

"*Nee*, it isn't quite time to do the feeding." They had always kept to a strict schedule when taking care of the animals. She'd always thought it was amazing how the horses and the two milk cows always knew when it was time for someone to feed them.

"I'll help you."

"*Denke*." She was quite capable of doing it, but it was nice that he offered. And they would get done quicker together.

Something she would need help with was getting more hay delivered and having someone stack it in the barn. She needed it to get them through the winter months.

She couldn't wait until the last moment to address it either. Her brother had always purchased hay from Mr. Schiller, but he had advanced in age until he no longer delivered hay on his big wagon. In truth, he didn't sell it anymore either.

"Do you know anyone I can buy hay from? We aren't out yet, but there isn't enough to make it through the winter."

He rubbed his chin. "Mr. Franks sells hay and delivers it, but he charges top dollar. I can ask around and see if anyone else will bring it for you."

"I'd appreciate that," she said. If that didn't work out, maybe she could find someone from the non-Amish community. They often posted notices at the mercantile of things and services they offered the Amish community.

The animals had to eat, and it was her job to make sure they didn't go hungry.

"I'll ask around," he said. "There have to be several people who sell hay. Most people don't put it up, and everyone needs it through the winter."

"At least I know where Ivan bought grain."

"Not too many places to get it," he said.

"I know." Only two places in the community sold bagged grain.

She couldn't afford to spend too much money on hay or anything else. And she had to get the business back up and running. She'd told the two men who worked for her brother that she needed two weeks to get everything in order before she wanted the workshop to resume.

Maybe she should have said one week instead. But it didn't matter now.

She hadn't been included in the family business, and she needed to go through the records and understand how things worked before it all started up again.

There was so much to do that it was overwhelming. She rubbed her eyes then went to get the coffee.

∿

Thomas volunteered to milk the two cows while she did the feeding. She gratefully accepted. The younger heifer was sometimes cranky and wanted to kick when being milked. But thank God, the animals had all survived the fire.

While Thomas was tending the milk cows, she fed and watered the horses, goats, and chickens. She collected the eggs, which were plentiful, and turned the horses out into the pasture after they finished their grain. She would bring them back into the smaller stock barn, which was the only barn she had left, in the evening before the temperature dropped for the night.

She would have to do the evening milking, too. It was the one job she hated. Maybe she would sell the cattle. There were three cows and the old bull, which she was afraid of. She had to go and fetch the milk cows twice a day if they weren't waiting to come in.

She hurried back to the milk shed where Thomas was finishing up.

"Do you know of anyone who might be interested in buying the cows?" she asked.

He glanced up from the milking stool. "Sure, if you really want to sell them. Mr. Schmidt would buy them in a minute. He's building a dairy herd. Not sure about the bull, but you could sell him for meat."

She laughed and said, "He'd be tough and flavorless, like he is in life." As much as he scared her, she didn't want to sell him to be butchered.

Thomas snorted. "I'll find someone to take him off your hands if you want me to. The cows, too."

She considered it for a second and said, "*Jah*, I'd rather buy some milk than have to deal with cattle."

"Honestly, I don't blame you," he said.

"I guess I'm not the milk maid type." There was no guessing about it.

"I'll talk to Mr. Schmidt and find a buyer for the bull."

"I appreciate it," she said. That would take care of one of her biggest headaches. The sooner they were sold, the better she would like it.

"Consider it done," he said.

They returned to the house to warm up and spent the rest of their visit in the kitchen where it was always warm and sweet-smelling from her cooking and baking. The kitchen was her favorite place in the house. It made her think of family and good food and contentment.

~

Four days passed before she spied Thomas coming down the driveway again. She'd become a little perplexed that he'd stayed away that long.

Maybe he didn't know it, but she needed him more now than ever. Needed to know he was there for her in hard times, too. He was a source of strength she could draw from. Not necessarily to help with chores, but at least to be there for moral support.

He stopped at the house and jumped out of the buggy.

She came out to greet him. A brisk wind whipped a few loose strands of dark blonde hair into her face. She brushed them away.

"Sorry I haven't been by. I've been really busy with work. But I wanted to let you know I've found a buyer for the bull. And Mr. Schmidt wants the cows. They should all be out of here in the next few days."

"*Denke*," she said, instantly feeling better about why he hadn't been there.

He glanced around.

"Would you like some *kaffe* to warm up?" she said.

"*Nee.* I have to go. I'm working on a home remodel, and I'm already late. I just wanted to stop in and let you know people would be coming to purchase the cattle."

Disappointment hit her hard. "I wish you could stay longer."

"I'll stop by in a couple of days and make sure the cattle are gone."

"Okay. *Denke* for helping with them," she said.

"You don't have to thank me."

She felt like she did. She felt very much like she needed to thank him for helping—which was odd because she'd never felt that way before.

"Anyway, I have to go," he said and climbed back into his buggy.

And just like that, he drove down the driveway and turned onto the main road.

∾

Later that afternoon, a crew of men came with a large wagon pulled by two huge black draft horses. They didn't stop at the house. They went straight to the rubble from the burned out barn and began loading it onto the wagon.

She didn't go to talk to them. It wasn't expected considering she'd lost two loved ones in the fire. But she watched from a distance for a while. The men worked efficiently, removing the larger pieces first, often having to work together to pick up large sections and moving them to the wagon.

She watched for a while, until the stink of the fire and charred wood got stirred up and drifted on the air. The stench brought it all back into focus more than watching the men clearing the area.

She went inside and watched from the parlor window. She wasn't sure why she felt compelled to watch the men removing the debris, but she intended to observe until the last load was taken out. It wasn't long before the first wagon load rumbled past the house, on the way to where they would dump the refuse.

As the first wagon load went out, a second wagon came in, this one pulled by two big sorrel horses. And so it continued throughout the day. One wagon was filled and rolled out and the second wagon pulled in to take its place.

The huge pile of rubble slowly grew smaller and smaller until it was almost cleared. The burn stink hung thick in the air, but it would dissipate soon enough.

She supposed another barn or workshop should be built on the spot even though the idea of it kind of bothered her. It was the place her brother and Jennifer had lost their lives in such a horrible manner.

She would think about it later. She was just happy to get the site cleaned up so the constant reminder wasn't right in everyone's face the moment they walked out the back door.

~

Three days later, an hour after she'd walked the children to school, Thomas showed up. This time he didn't even get out of the buggy.

"Did the *menner* come for the cattle?" He hadn't even said *gut morning* to her.

"*Jah*, the *menner* came yesterday and took them," she said. "*Denke* for making the arrangements."

"*Gut.* I'm glad that's settled," he said. "I found a *mann* who will deliver hay. He'll be getting in touch with you."

"Thank goodness," she said. He had just lifted another weight off her shoulders.

He fidgeted. "I wanted to talk to you about something."

A strange feeling struck her, and she was suddenly certain he was going to say something unpleasant.

"What?"

"I thought I could deal with all of this," he said. "I thought I could deal with the responsibilities you've been saddled with.

But I'm afraid it's going to be too much. I want to call off our courtship."

She gaped at him. *"What?"*

"I'm sorry. My timing is not *gut*. But I... Well, I just don't see how this is going to work."

"I don't understand..." Her stomach twisted, and she felt her throat tighten.

"I want to call off our courtship." He spoke slowly as if she were a child.

She blinked hard, unable to believe what she was hearing. "But I just lost my brother and his wife."

"I know that," he said, somewhat impatiently now. "I know that. I can't help that, can I?"

She stared at him. Could he really be so callous?

"Do you understand what I'm saying?" He shifted nervously in his seat.

"Of course, I understand," she snapped. She felt tears threatening to spill down her face. She was not going to let the tears fall in front of him.

"I guess you'd better be on your way then," she added coldly.

He just looked at her.

"Please *go*," she said. She willed her tears away.

He clucked to the horse, and just like that, he drove out of her life.

For a moment, she watched him go. In an odd way, it felt like she was in a dream state, except she knew she wasn't. She'd just been dumped by the man whom she'd thought loved her.

Shaking uncontrollably, she rushed inside the house and fell into a kitchen chair. She covered her face with her hands and let the tears come.

What a horrid, horrid man. She couldn't believe he'd broken off their courtship because of her responsibilities. Wasn't that what he'd said? What was wrong with him? What kind of man was he?

She cried it out then swiped at her eyes. They felt puffy, and she couldn't breathe.

"F-Fine," she managed to whisper. She didn't need anyone like that in her life. She would cope on her own. She didn't need a man who wasn't strong enough to handle the responsibilities she'd had put upon her.

She would handle them herself, and she would take care of the children. And nothing and no one would stop her.

Chapter Three

The following morning was gray and cold as she walked with Anna and Peter to school. Anna held her hand in a tight grip as she had ever since the fire.

Peter walked quietly as if lost in thought.

Peter had liked it when Thomas came and visited. Sometimes Thomas had taken him and Anna for buggy rides that they'd all enjoyed.

Sarah had told them the night before that she and Thomas were no longer courting,

and he wouldn't be coming back.

Anna had nodded, but Peter asked a bunch of questions. She had been very careful not to lay blame on Thomas, even though that was where the blame belonged. Still, she had no desire to make the children angry with him.

But in truth, he had called it off because he was a weak man. Simple as that. He wasn't mean or hateful, and though he'd broken her heart, she could not, would not resent him. After sleeping on it, she was glad she'd found out he had no spine before she married him.

He'd done her a favor. Brokenhearted or not, she would not deny reality. And at the moment, getting the business going was her top priority. They had to have income.

She'd gotten a decent amount for the cattle, but that wouldn't last long if nothing else was coming in. And she and the children had to survive. Therefore, the business did, too.

"We're almost there," she said when the school came into view.

⁓

By the time she got home, the temperature had dropped a few degrees, and the air felt heavy. Sarah was sure it was going to snow before the children were finished with school for the day.

She put on a pot of coffee and started cleaning the parlor. About thirty minutes into her routine, she glanced out the window and saw a buggy coming up the driveway.

Who was here? She wasn't expecting anyone. She watched through the window until the buggy drew close enough that she saw the bishop.

What in the world was he doing here? It must be something important. She hurried to the door to greet him. She opened the door and waited for him.

"Bishop Yoder, what brings you out on this blustery day?"

"We're having a community meeting to discuss the situation with the Fisher's *kinner*."

"What?" she said.

What was he talking about?

"We must meet to talk about what's best for the *kinner*. You need to come, too. We're meeting at the Braun's place in their basement where they hold preaching service when it's their turn. We'll be there at one o'clock to decide what we should do."

"I-I don't understand," she said. Her heart beat so hard it slammed in her chest, and she heard the thumping in her ears along with a strange ringing sound.

"Sarah, I'm not sure this is the best situation for you or the *kinner*. You're a mere seventeen years old. We have to talk about this and come to an agreement about this situation."

"But I can care for them. We're *familye*," she said in a rising, frightened voice.

"I understand you wish to care for them. But I think it's best to have a community discussion about the situation. We don't want to leave you stranded in a situation you can't manage. You'll all suffer. Please plan to attend this afternoon."

And before she could protest further, he said, "We'll see you at one." Then he turned and hurried to his buggy as the first fat snowflakes fluttered down.

She stood there holding the door in a state of shock. As he drove back down the driveway, she finally closed the door. They couldn't take the children from her ... could they?

Sarah had barely retreated into the house before she heard another buggy coming up the driveway.

She hurried to look out the parlor window facing the driveway to see who it was. She instantly recognized the horse as belonging to Rebecca. Still reeling from the bishop's visit, she went to the door to let Rebecca in.

Rebecca climbed down and practically ran to the front door. She was red-faced and panting for breath.

"What's the matter," Sarah said. Clearly something was wrong.`

"Sarah, I came to warn you. The bishop is planning to meet with you about the *kinner*."

"He was just here."

"*Ach, nee*," Rebecca said.

"They think I can't take care of the *kinner*," Sarah said, tears coming to her eyes.

Rebecca wrung her hands. "What are you going to do?"

"I don't have much of a choice," Sarah said. "I have to go meet with them this afternoon."

And who knew what was going to happen during that meeting.

~

Sarah was a nervous wreck when she arrived at the Braun's place. They ushered her into the basement where at least thirty other community members had gathered to discuss the situation.

Almost all of them stared at her as she came down the stairs. She felt like she'd been placed on display to be gawked at. Warmth filled her cheeks. What did these people think of her? That she wasn't grown-up enough to care for her own niece and nephew?

They were wrong.

She reached the bottom step and looked around, unsure what was expected of her.

"Sarah, please sit." Bishop Yoder indicated some free chairs with a sweep of his hand.

She took one of the folding metal chairs and felt like a bug on display as everyone looked between her and the bishop.

"Now that Sarah's here," Bishop Yoder said, "we may as well start the discussion. We have enough people here from the community."

A few people nodded, and there was a low murmur that ran through the group.

Sarah's stomach twisted into knots. What was going to happen?

"We're here to talk about what's best for the Fisher *kinner* who are now eleven and nine years old. Sarah is seventeen."

"Too young," someone said in a low voice.

She wasn't too young. She felt like saying it out loud, but now wasn't the time to speak out. She needed to hear what they had to say before she stated her own thoughts on the matter.

"It's best to keep *kinner* with *familye*," old Mr. Schiller said in a matter-of-fact tone.

"But only if they can do the job," a middle-aged man said. Sarah didn't recognize him at all.

"The girl's old enough to get married if she wanted to. In which case she could become a mother soon enough," Mr. Burger said. "I don't see why she can't run the *haushold*."

"She has to be able to provide for all of them," the bishop said.

"They had a business. Why can't she run that?" Mr. Martin said.

She could run the business. She just needed to get it going again. The workers were ready to come back. They were just waiting for her to give them the go-ahead.

"I think we have to consider what's best for all of them," Bishop Yoder said. "And that includes Sarah. I honestly don't see how she can manage everything without driving herself into exhaustion. And that won't be *gut* for any of them."

Sarah's heart pounded so hard she was surprised they couldn't hear it. It felt like it was trying to break out of her chest. This wasn't going well at all.

The bishop continued, "I think it would be best if Peter and Anna went to live with families who are willing to take in one more child."

What? Split them up? It would be bad enough if they both went to live with another family. But splitting them up...no, they couldn't do that.

"Sarah could manage the woodworking shop," the bishop said. "And when Sarah is a bit older and things are more stable, the *kinner* can go back home with her."

A few people nodded agreement, while some others verbally agreed. But a few were clearly against the arrangement.

Sarah stood up. "Please, everyone. I'm asking you to give me a chance to prove I can manage the workshop and the *kinner*. I think most, if not all of you, know I lost my parents when I was young. My brother and his *fraa* gave me a home and all the love I needed to thrive. I'm not sure I would have done well at all if I had been placed in a stranger's home, or even with someone I knew. I needed *familye* like I never had before. They gave me what I needed. I can give my *bruder's kinner* the same love and guidance. They need me. And I need them, too. Please don't pull my *familye* apart. I know I can do this."

Her heart raced even harder as the people stared at her then broke into quiet discussion among themselves.

Bishop Yoder stared at her intently. Finally, he said, "It goes against my better judgment, but I suppose it wouldn't hurt to give it a trial period. Let's give it through Christmas Day and reevaluate then."

"*Denke*," Sarah said as relief rolled through her. "I promise I can do this."

Now she just had to make sure everything went right so the community members couldn't use anything against her.

She couldn't wait to get home, have some hot chocolate, and try to relax a bit before she went to get the children and walk them home from school. She didn't want to be wound up like she was. They were intelligent children and would pick up that something was off with her.

And that brought about the question of whether she should tell the children what was going on. She hated the idea of keeping something like this from them. But on the other hand, there was nothing to be gained from telling them and upsetting them and letting them worry.

She could worry enough for all of them. Maybe she should just stay quiet. But what if one of the children from school got wind of it and told them? They wouldn't know what was going on, and they might even be upset with her for not telling them.

The more she thought about it, the more she realized there was a real possibility of them finding out from a classmate. That settled it. She had to tell them.

Maybe that would be for the best anyway. They were very helpful, but if they knew something this big was happening, they would do everything they could to make sure they were allowed to stay with her.

She would tell them after supper. It was the right thing to do given the circumstances.

That evening, after they had eaten and Sarah and Anna had done the dishes, Sarah made a large pan of hot chocolate and called everyone into the parlor where the potbelly stove had warmed the room until it was cozy.

She passed out the mugs of chocolate.

"I must tell you *kinner* something. I need you to listen to everything I have to say. Then you can ask me any questions you may have. All right?"

"*Jah*," Anna said.

Peter nodded, but there was a doubtful look on his face.

She told them what had happened at the meeting, sparing no detail.

When she finished, Peter looked angry. "How can they want to do that to us?"

"They aren't doing it out of meanness," Sarah said. "They just want everything to be as *gut* for all of us as possible. They're just afraid that you won't get the home you need. You can't blame them for being concerned about us."

Peter didn't look like he believed it, and Anna looked frightened.

"Don't worry. It'll be fine," Sarah said. "We'll just have to make sure it goes well. Then *nee* one can say anything."

Chapter Four

✥

"Sarah," Marcus Byler said, "I borrowed Mr. Miller's phone so I could check on the wood shipment. Seems they're delayed on the cherry wood, and it's holding up the shipment."

"*Ach, nee*," Sarah said. "Did he say when it's going to be shipped?"

"Next Wednesday," he said.

"That's over a week. This is not *gut*," she said. "We're going to be even more behind."

"I know," Marcus agreed. "We better do some small jobs. It's better than sitting around waiting for the shipment for the big renovation job."

"I agree," she said. Some work was better than none. But it wasn't going to pay nearly as well. The delay would cause an instant financial strain. The workers depended on their pay coming on time, and they'd already lost two weeks' pay before she called them back to work.

They were good workers and had quickly caught up on the waiting orders.

"Well, there's nothing we can do about it," she said. "We'll just have to do as much as we can and work around the problem."

Thank goodness she'd sold the cattle. Not only had she gotten rid of the headache of having to deal with them, but she now needed some of that money to pay the workers. She couldn't —she wouldn't ask them to wait for their pay. She'd already inconvenienced them.

It also wouldn't look good to the bishop and community members who'd wanted to split up the children. No. She needed everything to go as well as possible.

⁓

The following morning, Sarah awoke suddenly. She was sure something had pulled her from sleep. She lay in her warm bed listening for any sound that was out of place, but the house was quiet.

She rubbed her eyes and glanced at the clock on the bedside stand. It was five minutes until five. Just minutes away from the alarm blaring her awake.

She got up and hurried through her morning routine before going to the kitchen and getting the fire started in the big stove. It would be nice to have a gas stove to go with the refrigerator. Maybe one day when the business was doing well, she would convert from the big old cookstove. Though she did appreciate the heat the cookstove produced in the winter for it made the kitchen a wonderful place to sit and drink coffee or read a book.

She got the woodstove going in the parlor along with the fireplace. The house would be toasty warm before Anna and Peter got up for breakfast.

She glanced out the window. It was still very dark out, but it would lighten some before they had to head out for school. And thankfully they hadn't had any real snowfall yet. They'd had a few flurries, but nothing had accumulated.

She started breakfast, frying bacon and scrambling eggs. Toast and butter would finish off the meal.

She could hear Peter up and getting ready for school. They would both be ready before she finished cooking. They were good at being on time.

A few minutes later, Peter came in. "I smell bacon. Yummy."

"And scrambled eggs," she said.

"My favorite breakfast." He perched at the table.

"I think it must be Anna's favorite, too." She listed for sounds of the little girl getting ready, but she didn't hear anything.

"Go make sure Anna is up. I don't want to be late getting to school." She turned the bacon over.

"Sure." Peter scampered off.

He raced back moments later. "She isn't here."

"What?" Sarah's heart lurched.

"She's gone," Peter said. "She must be outside."

"Put your boots and coat on and go see if you can find her. She must be in the small barn with the animals." Anna loved the barn cats. She must have gone to see them. Or the horses. She loved them as well. Yes, she had to be there. It was too cold to go much further if she didn't have to.

Anna was much like her when it came to the cold. Winter could be very beautiful to look at, but not so much fun when a person had to spend a lot of time out in it.

Peter got his boots on and buttoned his coat. "I'll be back in a minute." He went out to look for his sister while she finished making their breakfast.

She looked at the clock. They should be back. The stock barn wasn't far from the house. Something was wrong. She set the food on back burners and hurried to put her outdoor clothes on. Why weren't they back?

She glanced out the window, but it was still too dark to see much. No lantern light glowed from the stock barn. But there shouldn't be anyway. It had been drilled into both children not to light the barn lanterns without an adult accompanying them, especially since the fire. But it wasn't so dark that she couldn't determine that no one was out there.

She rushed outside.

It was very quiet. Then she spied Peter running toward her. She raced to meet him.

"I can't find her anywhere," he said. "She isn't in any of the buildings. She isn't here."

Panic nearly flattened Sarah. What was she going to do? She could have Peter run to the neighbors and put out a call for help, but that might have catastrophic consequences with the bishop. On the other hand, not asking for help might also place Anna in jeopardy, and Sarah couldn't do that no matter what happened as a result.

"I bet I know where she is," Peter said suddenly.

"Where?"

"The Kauffman's got a new cart pony for their *kinner,* and Anna thinks he's beautiful. I bet she snuck over there to see him."

Oh, dear God, please let her be there. "Let's go. We have to find her. If she isn't there, we must get people to help search for her."

Lord. What if she'd fallen into a pond or the creek? She couldn't swim very well, and the water would be freezing.

They didn't walk, they ran over the fields until Sarah's side ached. She didn't stop. She pushed herself until they caught sight of the Kauffman's big red barn.

"There look! There she is," Peter said between his panting breaths.

Anna stood at the fence and a lovely gray pony stood on the other side letting her stroke his neck.

Sarah nearly collapsed with relief.

"Anna," she called. "We have to get home for breakfast. You're going to be late to school."

Anna turned from the fence and ran to them.

"Anna, you scared me half to death," Sarah said.

"I'm sorry, *Aenti*. I just wanted to see the pony."

"I know," Sarah said. "But we didn't know where you were. We were afraid something bad had happened to you. Don't ever do that again. We could have walked over together after school. Now you're going to be late on top of scaring us."

Anna looked at the ground. "I'm sorry. I won't do it again."

Sarah patted her back. She wanted to pick her up and hug her, but she wanted the lesson to sink in.

She said a silent prayer of thanks that Anna was all right. Things could have turned out horribly different. The child had no idea of the disaster her adventure could have caused.

Sarah rubbed her temple where the first signs of a headache were developing. "Come on, let's get home and have some breakfast. Then we have to get to school. I'll harness the horse while you eat, or else you're going to be truly late."

And she didn't need that. Not when the bishop and others were looking for an excuse to break them up and put them in other homes.

Peter glanced at her as if he had some idea what she was thinking. He took her hand and gave it a squeeze. She smiled at him. He was a bright child and very well might realize the depth of the situation. They couldn't afford any mess ups. Too much was riding on things going right.

～

Sarah poured herself a cup of tea and sat at the table. Somehow, she had gotten the children to school with exactly two minutes to spare before the bell was rung. She pushed the horse into the fastest trot he could give to get them there on time.

When she got home, she cooled him down and put him in his stall to keep him from getting cold. Then she hurried to the house and just collapsed from the scare she'd had.

Thankfully, the kitchen was still warm, and the tea was good and hot.

She would dust and sweep, but not until she had some time to think about what had happened. She didn't like the position she found herself in. If anything went wrong, and anyone found out, it would be leverage to use against her. They needed to be very careful until the bishop was satisfied that she was capable of managing the household and the business.

She was deep into her thoughts when a light rap on the door pulled her out of thoughts of disaster.

Thomas Stolz, one of her woodworkers stood on the steps.

"Thomas, come in," she said.

He waved his hand. "I just wanted to let you know that circumstances have come up with my *familye*, and well... I'm sorry, but I'm going to have to move my *familye* back to Pennsylvania as soon as possible. I want to get settled there before Christmas. I really hate to leave you in a bind. But I must quit now in order to get us packed and ready to move as quickly as possible."

His words hit her like a punch to the gut.

"*Ach*," she said, her mind reeling. "I'm really sorry to hear you have to go. But I-I understand. I'll write out your check."

"*Denke*, Sarah."

"Are you sure you don't want to come in?"

"*Nee*. I'll wait."

She nodded then went to write his check. Now what was she going to do?

She hurried back to give him his pay. "*Denke*, for all the *wunderbar* work you did here. If you want me to write a letter to help you get a new job, I'd be happy to do that for you."

"That would be *wunderbar*. I didn't want to ask you for one, after having to leave like this. But I would appreciate it if you did."

"Stop by tomorrow, and I'll have one waiting for you." She smiled even though she was in inner turmoil.

"*Denke*, Sarah. I'll see you tomorrow."

She nodded, and he turned and hurried to his buggy.

She closed the door and rubbed her forehead.

As bad as it was, she couldn't let this stop her. She had to hire someone quickly. She would have to go to the mercantile and pin up a job opening notice on the cork board. Hopefully, someone with excellent skills would see it and apply soon.

She would handle the situation. She had to. And she wouldn't fail. Because that would be failing her brother, and she wouldn't do that, no matter what.

Chapter Five

The following morning, Sarah had already written the letter of recommendation for Thomas before she prepared breakfast. At least she had that done before she walked Anna and Peter to school. By the time they reached the school, thick clouds had gathered overhead. The temperature had warmed a little overnight, taking it a little above freezing, so it was likely going to rain. Hopefully, she would make it home before it cut loose and drenched her.

But that was a hope that didn't pan out. Halfway home, the first fat drops of rain hit her. Then a steady rain began falling in earnest. A little further down the road and the heavens had opened with the intention of flooding the earth a second time. Rain came down in sheets, soaking her until water was running off her in rivulets.

She sighed with exasperation. She couldn't seem to get a break these days. She shivered in her soaked clothing and hurried as fast as she could without running.

When she finally got home, she pulled off her clothes and, after changing into a dry dress, she hung the wet clothes in the basement to dry. Chilled to the bone, she went to the kitchen and made tea. She stoked the fire in the cookstove and settled at the table.

The house was spotless so there was no need for anything other than keeping the kitchen clean for the day. She just wanted to get warm and lose herself in the silence for a while. Then she'd head to the workshop and check on things there.

Later, she should work on the quilt she'd started just before the fire, but she didn't want to. Not yet. She took a sip of her tea and worked to think of things to be grateful for.

~

By the time she had to leave to fetch the children home, she felt tired and drained, which was ridiculous since she hadn't even finished her work yet. It had continued raining off and on, so she wasn't able to finish her outside chores. In truth, she was having trouble motivating herself to do anything. This was unlike her, but there was no denying that she just wanted to stay warm in the kitchen.

The two men running the workshop didn't need her after she'd checked in, so she hadn't stayed long.

She debated harnessing the horse and driving to pick up Peter and Anna but decided against it. She could be well on her way by the time she got the horse groomed, harnessed and hitched to the buggy.

She gathered their umbrellas in case it started raining again and set off on foot. By the time she'd walked a quarter of the way, she was so exhausted that she wished she'd harnessed the horse. Too late to worry about that now, however. She would just have to keep going, tired or not.

She slogged on, but the longer she walked, the worse she felt until she was forced to admit she was coming down with something.

Sarah finally made it to the school, and the children ran to greet her. She did her best to appear cheery. The idea of walking home exhausted her before they even started. But at least, it wasn't raining.

They hadn't made it very far before she heard a buggy coming up behind them. She turned and relief spread through her as the buggy caught up and stopped.

Rebecca cried out, "Get in. I'll give you a ride home."

"I'm really glad to see you," Sarah said.

Peter and Anna climbed into the back, and Sarah climbed up beside Rebecca.

"You look exhausted," Rebecca said. "Are you all right?"

"I think I'm coming down with something. I honestly didn't know if I was going to make it home."

"Sarah, you've got to take better care of yourself. The *kinner* depend on you."

"I know."

"I'll get you home in a jiffy," Rebecca said. "Then you need to lie down."

Sarah chuckled. "Not until I get the chores done and feed the *kinner*. Then I can lie down for a while."

"I have a better idea," Rebecca said. "The *kinner* and I will do the chores. Then I'll make supper while you rest."

"That sounds more than *wunderbar*. But I can't have you do all that."

"*Jah,* you can," Rebecca said. "That way you'll have some time to relax and maybe by morning, you'll feel a lot better."

Sarah sure hoped she would feel better by morning. "I really appreciate that."

≈

Sarah made a fire in the wood stove in the parlor and lay down on the sofa. She wished she could go to bed, but she wouldn't do that until the children were ready for bed.

She listened to Rebecca fixing a meal for Peter and Anna while the kids laughed and talked with her.

Rebecca was good with children. She'd grown up with six younger siblings, and she had helped take care of them since she was small.

Sarah smiled at their chatter and laughter.

Rebecca popped in. "I'm making a pot of chicken noodle soup for you. Would you like some now or should I put it in the refrigerator when it's done?"

"You didn't have to go to all that trouble," Sarah said. Yet, it was just like Rebecca.

"I know I didn't have to, but I wanted to. You shouldn't be trying to cook. I'm going to prepare some things in the refrigerator for the *kinner*."

Sarah let out her breath in a long sigh. "I sure appreciate it."

Rebecca waved her hand. "That's what friends are for. Shall I bring you a bowl of soup then?"

"I don't feel like eating tonight," Sarah said.

"Then I'll put the soup away, and you can warm some when you feel like eating."

No matter how bad things got, there was at least one person she could count on. It felt good to have Rebecca there with them, if only for a little while.

~

Sarah awoke the following morning hot with fever and a general feeling of being unwell. Overwork, worry, and stress all had a hand in dragging her down.

She felt much too awful to take the children to school. And she wasn't about to let them go alone and walk down the side of a busy road. She hated that they would miss school, maybe more than once.

It wasn't good for them. And it wouldn't be good for her if the bishop found out they were missing school. But the risk of walking the highway outweighed her fear of them missing class. If she couldn't take them, they couldn't go.

She would have told them to cut across the neighbors' properties to bypass the road, but the neighbors had cattle and a bull turned out where they would have to walk. Bulls were just as dangerous as the highway, maybe more so in her opinion, so that wasn't an option.

As soon as she felt better, she would harness the horse and drive them to school. She wasn't sure when she would feel well enough to walk that far.

Over the next three days, she only got up when she had too. She stayed on the sofa, and she was thankful Rebecca had prepared enough food for Peter and Anna. She wasn't at all sure she would have been able to pull meals together for them.

Peter came in at noon. "Would you like us to heat up the soup for you?"

"Maybe a bit." She wasn't hungry, but she knew she had to eat.

Peter had taken charge. He warmed food for her, himself and his sister. They were taking care of the animals twice a day. She'd even heard them cleaning up without being asked. They were doing everything they could to help her. But she feared not everyone would be happy about the situation.

∾

On the fourth day, the bishop showed up.

She managed to get to the door, and immediately wished she hadn't. The look of alarm on his face told her how bad she looked—and that he was concerned for all of them.

"My dear, do you need a doctor?"

"*Nee,* I'm just a little under the weather. Getting better every day." She didn't feel like she was getting better, but what else could she say?

"May I come in?"

With her heart beating much too fast at his unexpected visit, she said, "*Ach, jah*, I'm sorry." She felt foolish. She stepped aside to allow him in and took him into the kitchen.

"Can I get you some *kaffe* or tea? I don't have any fresh pie or cake." She forced herself to be as natural as possible.

"*Nee*, but *denke*," he said. "I heard the *kinner* had missed school, and you missed preaching service. I knew something had to be wrong. Are you sure you're on the mend?"

"*Jah*, and my dear friend Rebecca Troyer prepared a lot of food for me and the *kinner*, so we've been fine."

He nodded. "Rebecca is a *wunderbar* young woman."

Thankfully, the children were playing quietly in one of the bedrooms upstairs. If they knew the bishop was there, and maybe they did, they wouldn't come out.

He glanced around as if searching for anything out of place.

"I have to tell you," he said. "I, and some of the elders, are concerned about your ability to cope with all of strain you're under."

"I'm afraid I caught a bug from the mercantile. A woman coughed in my face two days before I came down ill." She wasn't lying. A woman had coughed on her when she'd stopped for milk and cheese. But she had no idea if the woman had been sick or not. One thing she was pretty sure of was that fevers didn't come from stress.

He nodded. "Well, I assume the *kinner* will be returning to school tomorrow?"

"Indeed, I'm very much on the mend," she said. She *had* planned for them to go to school the following day.

"All right, then, take it easy so you make a full recovery," he said.

"I will."

She showed him out and watched him drive down the driveway to the main road. Her banging heart finally slowed to a more normal pace.

What if the bishop changed his mind and expected her to allow the children to go to other families right away instead of waiting until the deadline? What could she do then?

Chapter Six

The weather had turned very cold, but Sarah was so happy that she had fully recovered from her illness that she didn't even mind the extra work the cold weather caused.

So far, her luck was holding. The bishop hadn't been back, nor had he said anything at the next preaching service, which they'd all attended. She was especially thankful for that.

Shortly after returning home from walking the children to school, someone knocked on the front door. This alerted her to know that whoever was there had never been to her place before. Everyone, except the bishop, knocked on the back door not the front.

She hurried to see who had come. To her surprise, it was a man she'd never seen before. He was strikingly handsome with piercing, deep blue eyes and dark blonde hair.

"Hello," she said.

"Are you Sarah Fisher?"

"*Jah*, I'm Sarah."

He looked surprised, and she assumed it was because he was expecting someone older. She couldn't blame him.

He recovered quickly. "I'm Daniel Miller. I saw the ad for a skilled woodworker. Is the position still open?"

Her heart leapt with joy. Finally, someone had responded to her ad.

"It is still open. I'm seeking someone who can help run the shop. I have two other workers. But they don't have the skills of the *mann* who had to leave. Would you like to come in for some *kaffe* and we can talk about it?"

"I can do that," he said.

"Come on in. I just made fresh *kaffe*."

He followed her to the kitchen.

"Make yourself comfortable," she said.

She brought him a mug and poured it full for him and refilled her own cup. "Help yourself to the cream and sugar."

"I take it black," he said.

She nodded and spooned in sugar and poured cream into her

own mug. "I'm sure you're wondering why someone so young has a business to run."

"It crossed my mind."

She quickly told him how she had come to live there with her brother and sister-in-law and how tragedy had struck a second time.

When she finished, he looked rather in awe. "I must say, you're a resilient young woman, and you should be applauded."

Her cheeks warmed at the unaccustomed praise. "*Denke.* But I'm just doing what I must do." She took a sip of coffee. "Tell me about yourself."

"I just recently moved here," he said. "It's just my son and me. I'm afraid I lost my *fraa* a year ago."

"*Ach,* I'm so sorry," she said. Her heart went out to him. How dreadful to be widowed so young.

"She's with the Lord. She was a *gut* woman."

She nodded, not sure of what else to say about it, if anything.

"So, we have moved here for a new start," he said. "I ran a woodworking shop for several years prior to moving, and I have a letter of recommendation from my employer, if you'd like to see it."

"I would," she said.

He plucked a folded paper from his pocket and handed it to her. The tips of their fingers brushed, and an electric current zinged through her. Startled, she glanced up at him. He looked as if he'd felt something, too.

She unfolded the paper and quickly read over a letter that outlined his skills and work ethic. If everything in the letter was true, and she had no reason to believe it wasn't, he was even better than Thomas. And Thomas had been very good.

This man sounded like the best thing that had come along in weeks. But could she afford to pay him what he probably wanted and deserved?

"You sound exactly like what I'm looking for." She handed the letter back. "I have to be honest. I don't know if I can afford you."

He smiled showing white, even teeth. "I'll be honest, too. I could probably make more money working for a couple people I've already talked with, but they are both a *gut* distance from where I'm staying. I value my time considerably for I spend as much as I can with my son. Your shop is fifteen minutes away. So let's talk and see what we can work out."

Heart racing, she met his blue gaze and prepared to negotiate.

～

Sarah still couldn't believe she'd managed to hire Daniel Miller. Apparently, his time was valuable to him. In truth, she wished she could pay him more. And if he delivered the kind of work she thought he could, then maybe, hopefully, she could give him more money as things improved.

In a strange sense, she felt like a turning point had just landed on her doorstep. And an unfamiliar confidence settled in. She hoped they earned enough that month so she could meet the payroll for all three men. She had to make it work.

Her brother's business had earned a reputation, and he had always enjoyed steady work. But with someone like Daniel, maybe once she was able to pull a little ahead, she could start looking for bigger jobs. Her brother had settled for word-of-mouth to find business, but maybe she could actively market the business and get more work orders.

She needed to study what the most successful woodworking businesses did to get new business. Whatever they were doing, she would do, too.

One thing she needed to do was let potential customers know the business was now capable of doing work of a more varied nature.

According to Daniel's former employer, Daniel was an artist with wood and could craft anything. She needed to think about it. There had to be new business opportunities in their community that they could fill. She just needed to figure out what they were.

Maybe they could make something the *Englisch* folks would really like. There was nothing wrong with doing regular business with the *Englisch* as well as their own community.

While she felt a little thrill at the idea of growing the business and succeeding, she was still nervous that maybe it would all end up falling apart around her.

~

Daniel started the very next morning. He seemed to instantly fit with the other men who'd greeted him with enthusiasm. They had probably been as worried as she had been.

But maybe things were turning around. They'd received the delayed shipment of hardwood several days earlier, and now they had someone who could not only work with the wood but also run the workshop.

A week passed in what seemed like the blink of an eye to Sarah.

She felt so encouraged that she had taken out her quilting supplies and had gone to work on the one she'd set aside after the fire. It was going to be pretty when she finished the teal and burnt orange pattern on the white background. The hours passed quickly and before she knew it, she'd made a good deal of progress.

She got up to put more wood in the stove when an idea so

simple struck her that she scolded herself for not thinking of it before.

Her brother's business had focused on home renovation jobs, including cabinets, which were good business. But there was a huge untapped market he'd overlooked or ignored. But she needed to be successful, and she was pretty sure she knew what they needed to do.

First, she would speak with Daniel and see what he thought before she let her idea run away with her. If he thought it didn't stand a chance of working, she would rather know now before she completely fell in love with the idea.

She forced herself to wait until the men took their lunch hour before she went out to the woodshop. She let herself into the warm building.

All three workers turned to see who'd come in. She smiled at all of them.

"Daniel, could I have five minutes of your time? I'd like to get your professional opinion on an idea I have."

"All right," he said. "Do you mind if I bring my sandwich?"

"Of course, I don't mind," she said.

He grinned. "*Denke*."

He walked with her back to the house.

"Would you like a cup of *kaffe*?" she said.

"*Nee, denke.* I have plenty in my thermos."

"Have a seat." She motioned toward the kitchen table.

He took a seat, and she sat opposite him. "I was working on a quilt this morning, and I got an idea. But I need to know what you think, since I would be counting on you for most of the work."

"Okay," he said and bit into his sandwich.

"I was wondering how you would feel if we expanded the shop to include making things like hope chests, blanket chests, and other furniture like dressers. But I want to target the *Englisch* market, so perhaps we would want to make the items more decorative to appeal to them."

He chewed slowly and looked as if he was turning the idea over.

"You would have to advertise to reach them," he said.

"I'm prepared to do that." She knew of a man who ran website pages to advertise for Amish merchants. She would hire him to make a page for them to display their merchandise. She would find other places to advertise as well.

"I think your *bruder* should already have done this."

Excitement burned through her. "So, you think it's a *gut* idea?"

"*Jah.* I do. It's not original, for others are already doing this, especially in Ohio and Pennsylvania. But around here, not so much. You might consider marketing cabinets for the *Englischers* as well. There's *nee* reason we can't make the kind they would prefer as well as the plain ones we sell in our community."

"You have *nee* idea how happy this makes me," she said.

"What would you like us to start with?" He finished his sandwich.

"What about the big chests?"

"I think those are a *gut* choice. People have loved those for years. If we make some of them ornate and some plain, I think we can cover all kinds of buyers. We'd be in time for Christmas, too."

"How do you feel about more custom furniture orders?" she said.

"Woodworking is all the same. I can make anything a customer might ask for. There's really *nee* reason not to take more orders. If business gets so *gut* that we can't keep up, you'll easily be able to afford another worker."

"True," she said. She couldn't even imagine doing so well that they would need four workers. But it sounded nice.

"So, let's do this," he said.

"*Denke.* Just let me know what you need, and I'll get it."

"I'll make a list. This won't be difficult."

"*Denke*," she said again.

"*Nee* reason to thank me. This is what I do. We should be able to turn out some nice chests quickly."

"This makes me so happy," she said.

His lips quirked up at the corners. "Expansion is *gut*. Like I said, your *bruder* should have already been doing this. I'll head back out unless you have more to discuss."

"*Nee*, that's all I wanted to talk about. *Denke* again."

He nodded and headed back out to finish his lunch in the woodshop.

She had to stop herself from running around the house. They were going to make it; she felt sure of it now.

Then she thought of the bishop again and much of the luster of her joy vanished. No amount of business success would matter if they took Anna and Peter from her.

⁓

During the following days, Sarah stayed out of the workshop and out of the workers' way. But she was busy thinking about what items they could make and where and how she could advertise their business.

The easiest place to advertise was the mercantile. She made an ad that took half a sheet of paper. She used a blue Sharpie for the lettering and did her best to make the ad noticeable by adding flourishes in the corners.

When she was satisfied with it, she harnessed the horse and drove into town to the mercantile. Most of the customers were people from their community, but some non-Amish people shopped there as well.

She needed to place ads like this in non-Amish stores, too. She would have to work that out later.

She left the buggy and went inside and grabbed a cart. Might as well pick up some supplies while she was there. She went to the notice board and pinned up her ad and then headed for the coffee aisle.

She grabbed a can of coffee and headed for the dry goods aisle. As she bent to pick up a package of sugar, she heard the bishop's voice. And to her surprise, he was talking to Daniel. She'd thought he was still back at the shop, but by then, it was lunchtime, so he must have decided to run some errands. She knew she shouldn't listen to their conversation, but something kept her rooted to the spot.

She had an uneasy feeling they were talking about her.

"I feel bad for her," the bishop said, and then continued, "But the first concern of course, is the *kinner*."

"Of course."

It sure sounded like they were talking about her.

"Caring for the *kinner* and trying to run the business is a lot for Sarah," the bishop said.

"It's an awful lot," Daniel said. "I agree with you."

"I'm glad you're hired on," the bishop said. "We welcome you to the community."

They were talking about her. *Both of them.*

And wasn't Daniel joining right in and judging her when he didn't even know her? Maybe hiring him had been a mistake after all.

Chapter Seven

Sarah was still upset with Daniel and the bishop—for the bishop had been talking about her in public. She stung at their unfair opinion of her. She felt deeply the stress everybody was putting on her, but she was determined to make Christmas special.

After taking Peter and Anna to school, she got the handsaw and took the small sled her brother had used to haul feed to the different animal's pens and pulled it over the frozen ground to the woods behind the house.

She sawed low hanging boughs from several cedar trees and stacked them on the sled. As she sawed, fat snowflakes began drifting down. By the time she had enough evergreen branches to decorate the house and the workshop, the snow was coming down hard, and the ground was nearly covered.

She looked around, enjoying the first real snow. She rubbed her hands together to warm them a bit, then she sawed off a last bough and put it on the sled.

She started back to the house and hummed Christmas tunes to herself. Even though she had worries on her mind, she could make the place look nice. And it would smell nice, too. She'd always loved decorating for Christmas. Maybe they only used evergreen branches, candles, and ribbon, but those simple things made beautiful arrangements.

She couldn't wait to get home and make it look nice for Anna and Peter before they came home. She wanted them to have a nice Christmas. She knew her brother and Jennifer had a few gifts for both children squirreled away. They would probably be the most cherished presents they ever received. She'd made some gifts for each of them, too.

They would have as good a holiday as she could give them, starting that afternoon when they came home to find their home decorated.

She finally made it back with her load of greenery. She set aside some for the workshop and took the rest of the boughs into the house.

She placed greenery on every windowsill and on a small table pushed against a wall. Then she fetched the white and cream-colored candles and arranged them among the evergreens. When she finished with the arrangements, she stood back and inspected her work.

Pleased with the results, she went to the woodshop to decorate. Daniel was there working on a lovely cedar chest.

She ignored him and placed the evergreen branches and candles. She was pretty sure none of the candles would ever be lighted, but that was fine. They still looked nice.

Daniel glanced at her, but she pretended not to notice. She was much too annoyed at overhearing him to acknowledge that she'd seen him looking at her.

She finished decorating and quickly went back to the house.

⌒

When Anna and Peter came home from school, Anna squealed with delight when she saw the decorations.

"Can we light the candles?" she asked and clapped her hands.

"*Jah*, but only I light them, okay?" Sarah said.

"How come?" Anna said.

"Because it's ... dangerous. I don't want you hurt," Sarah said. After the catastrophic fire, Sarah wondered whether she'd ever feel easy about lighting a match again.

"Okay," Anna said, though she looked confused, for she'd lit candles before.

Sarah took a box of matches, and she lit each candle.

"They're so pretty," Anna said.

"Peter, keep an eye on those candles while I do the evening chores," Sarah said.

"All right," Peter said.

She shook her head and smiled. He was such a little gentleman. "*Denke*, Peter."

He grinned and said, "You're welcome."

⁓

Sarah and Peter went out to the workshop after the crew had gone home for the evening. She wanted to see how far Daniel had gotten with a few of the pieces he was working on. She was still too annoyed with him to go out while they were working. If one of them needed her for something, they knew they were welcome to come to the house.

"These are nice," Peter said and ran his hand over one of the chest lids.

"They are," she said. "Daniel does *wunderbar* work." Too bad she couldn't say the same thing about his character. Nice people didn't talk behind their backs about the person who had given them a job.

Still, Daniel was making the kinds of things that could really open up the business. So annoyed or not, she would keep her mouth shut and just go on about her duties. Besides, she didn't need to have a sour attitude. It was difficult enough. She didn't like conflict with anyone.

"Let's go back inside," she said. "I just wanted to see how they were coming along."

Peter reached for her hand. She smiled at him and squeezed his hand. They walked up the back porch and Sarah opened the side door. An ear-splitting scream, followed by another and another came from the parlor.

"Anna?" Sarah raced through the house.

Anna stood with her hand held out from her body, tears streaming down her face as sobs ripped from her. Her hand was red and already forming a big blister. The matches lay scattered on the floor around her.

She had been trying to light the other candles.

"Let me see your hand," Sarah said as she rushed to Anna.

The little girl further stretched out her hand.

"This needs to be seen by a doctor," Sarah said. There was no way she could properly treat a burn this severe.

"Peter, get a couple heavy blankets. I'll get the buggy. We must go to the medical center in town."

"We aren't going to Maggie Zook?" Peter said, clearly wondering why they wouldn't go to the herb woman who lived not far from their house.

"*Nee*. I... I don't want the bishop or any of the church elders finding out."

Peter nodded. "I'll get the blankets."

"I'm going for the buggy," Sarah said.

~

Even with the blankets, the ride into town was cold. But worse than the cold were the memories of her brother and Jennifer losing their lives in the barn fire. She couldn't stop thinking about it.

When they arrived, they were the only Amish at the clinic. The few *Englisch* people in the waiting room kept staring at them. Everyone knew the Amish people typically went to an herb woman, so their being at the clinic was a bit of an oddity.

Anna had sniffled the entire way there—not that Sarah blamed her. Thankfully, they didn't have to wait long to be seen. The doctor wanted to know how she had gotten burned, and Anna said, "I was trying to light the Christmas candles."

"Well, young lady, next time, let your mother do that for you. Okay?"

Anna's expression turned stricken. But of course, the doctor wouldn't know that Sarah was Anna's aunt, not her mother.

Anna looked up at Sarah with wide, grief-stricken eyes.

The doctor cared for the wound as gently as he could and then gave Sarah instructions on how to care for it at home.

After she paid their bill, they returned to the buggy and wrapped themselves in the blankets before heading home.

Now what? What if the bishop or the elders found out? Perhaps Sarah was being a bit too cautious, but she couldn't help it. Every day that passed, her anxiety about having the children taken away from her grew greater.

What was Anna going to tell the schoolteacher? There was no way Anna could miss any more school. Sarah would just have to say Anna had been hurt in a candle accident. She couldn't make up a story. She couldn't teach Anna that it was all right to lie.

But Sarah didn't regret going to the *Englisch* doctor. The less people in their community knew, the better.

Chilling cold rolled over her that had nothing to do with the night temperature. They simply couldn't take the children away from her. She *couldn't* give them up.

She clucked to the horse, and they set off at a fast trot. Now she just wanted to get home and get the children to bed. She didn't need any more problems or stress. But things kept coming her way regardless. Maybe she was being tested. If so, she was surely failing miserably.

Chapter Eight

Daniel was glad to get to the workshop and out of the biting cold. He unharnessed his horse and put him in the barn with the other workers' horses.

Sarah had insisted all their horses be kept inside through the day while they worked—at least during the cold snap. She seemed a kind person. He unharnessed Jack, and led him inside, then hurried to the workshop.

He'd heard about little Anna's accident and rubbed his temple. He was truly beginning to realize how much Sarah had been working to take good care of the children and keep the business going.

Looking back, he regretted agreeing with the bishop about her and the children. In truth, Daniel hadn't actually agreed with him. He'd more or less agreed with the bishop in a show of solidarity since he was a newcomer to the district.

But now he was disgusted by his blithe agreement. He had only been thinking of himself at the moment. Sarah had given him a job—a good one, too. She even cared about his horse. And all she wanted was to take care of those two children and run the business to support them.

And he had allowed his own selfishness to sway his comments.

He'd started to wonder if she somehow knew what he'd done. She had been open and friendly when he'd first started working there. But after he'd gone along with the bishop, she avoided him. And when she couldn't avoid him, her green eyes spoke of distrust. Had she somehow overheard him? No, that didn't seem possible. Still...

He'd even heard the other two workers saying something was wrong because she never came out to talk to them anymore. He was almost positive he was the thing that was wrong.

Maybe he could make up for it. Fix it somehow. And in turn, he wouldn't have to feel so lousy about himself for what he'd done.

He would do his best to make up for his words, starting right after work. Though he wasn't a fool. If she had gotten wind that he'd talked behind her back, she might not be very welcoming of his offer to help around the place.

~

Around noon a diesel truck pulled into the driveway. Sarah heard the rumble of the engine before she went to the window to see what was happening.

The truck pulled a long wagon stacked high with hay. Thank goodness, the hay had arrived.

She hurried to pull on her coat so she could show the driver where to take the load and then help stack it in the shed. She already had the check made out and she snatched it off the counter. Four-hundred dollars for one-hundred bales. But as bad as the price was, she knew it could go for as high as six dollars a bale.

Considering that they delivered it and helped stack it, she couldn't complain about the price. The driver had stopped and was waiting for her. His window was partly down. He had two big brawny young men crammed in with him. They must be the loading and unloading crew. Most likely, his sons by the look of them.

"You Miz Fisher?" he asked.

"*Jah*, I am."

"You expecting this big load of hay?"

"*Jah*. I need it taken to that shed."

"Okay. We'll just need you to show us where you want it stacked, though it don't look none too big from here," he said.

She was thankful that she wouldn't have to help stack it. The bales were very large so they would weigh a lot. She hurried to the shed and the man and his sons began tossing hay off the truck into a stack.

She rolled back the door. "Just bring it in here and stack it along the wall. And *denke* so much for bringing it for me."

"It's no problem. This is our business. It's what we do for people. If you need more hay, don't hesitate to call."

"I'll need more when this runs out," she said. "I'll call when I'm ready for another load."

"Okay, ma'am. We'll bring it as soon as you call."

She got out of their way and watched them take the hay into the shed.

She waited until they had all the hay off the wagon and had rumbled back down the driveway. That was one more thing off her list of items that had to been done. It was good to check one off instead of adding one.

She walked slowly back toward the house. There was so much to be done, she didn't know if she would ever get everything taken care of.

She would do her best. That was all a person could do. Life had been so much easier when her brother was there. She hadn't realized how good she'd had it. Well, none of that mattered now, because responsibility for everything lay on her shoulders.

～

Daniel waited until they closed up for the night, then he went to the house and tapped on the door.

Sarah answered a moment later.

"Is something wrong?" she said.

He fidgeted. "*Nee*. I just thought I'd stop over and see if you needed any help with anything. Not for pay. I just wanted to see if you needed something."

"Why?" she said frankly.

Should he just tell her? Maybe that would be best. Besides, they were supposed to be honest. He'd already been somewhat dishonest to seem more a part of the community.

He shifted from foot to foot. "I think you know I have a big mouth sometimes," he said.

She frowned. "What are you talking about?"

"Look, let's be honest. I said something to the bishop that I had *nee* right to say. I think you know about it by now."

She lifted her eyebrows. "Something about agreeing with the

bishop on a topic you don't truly understand. And that's none of your business."

He *knew* it. "*Jah*," he said. "That's what I'm talking about."

"*Denke* for bringing it up," she said. "Do you mind telling me why you did it?"

He felt really stupid having to explain why he'd opened his big mouth in the first place. "I'm new here, you know. And I wanted to fit in with the community. I know. That is no excuse. It got the better of my judgment." He could have kicked himself for what he'd said. "I am sorry for it."

"It's over now," she said. "You might as well forget about it."

"So can I do anything to help you out?" he said.

"*Nee,* I don't need any help, but *denke* for asking."

"Okay, then." He smiled despite himself. He would just keep asking until she let him help her with something.

He stopped and made the same offer over the next three afternoons, and each time, she rejected his offer. But he wasn't dissuaded in the least. He was going to make up for his stupidity.

The next afternoon, he stopped once again, and this time she said, "If you can repair a drawer, I could use your help."

"I can do that," he said.

"All right then. Come on in."

He went inside to the kitchen.

"It's in here," she said. "Peter pulled it out too far, then tried to jam it back in and the front came loose."

He pulled the drawer all the way out and took it to the table. He had the front back on in no time at all. "There, *gut* as new."

"*Denke*," she said. "Would you like a cup of *kaffe*?"

"I'd love a cup," he said.

"I'll make some," she said. "Have a seat."

He sat at the table.

She put some coffee on the stove and got mugs, sugar, and creamer out before she sat down across from him.

"So, what brought you to this district?" she said.

"I needed a change after I was widowed. But I still have *familye* in Pennsylvania, so I didn't want to move too far away. I knew a couple of people who'd lived here a *gut* while back, and they spoke highly of it. So here I am."

"That's as *gut* a reason as any other," she said.

"How's Anna's hand coming along?"

"It's much better. Not healed, but it feels better. I don't think she'll have scarring. Thank the *gut* Lord," she said.

"I'm glad to hear it. I guess the bishop or elders didn't say anything?"

"I haven't heard anything from them. So, I guess that's *gut* news," she said.

He nodded. "I'm certain the *kinner* are doing very well with you. *Nee* one should be trying to interfere. You're *familye*. And *familye* is always better than placing *kinner* with others."

"I couldn't agree more," she said. "Taking the kinner wouldn't be helping. That much is for sure and for certain."

She was braver than he'd originally thought. She was shouldering more weight than several men he knew. He couldn't help but be fascinated with her. Strong, pretty, family oriented. She had a lot to offer the right man.

How was this girl only seventeen, as he'd heard? She had a lot to take on and do by herself. If he was a betting man, which he wasn't, he would place money on her being successful in the long run.

"The *kaffe's* hot," she said and went get the pot. She filled their mugs. "Help yourself if you want the sugar and creamer."

"Sugar will be fine."

She smiled a little. "I remember, you like it black. That's a little too much for me. I like mine sweet and loaded with cream."

"We all have our ways," he said. "Doesn't mean one is better than the other."

"I suppose you're right about that," she said.

"When I'm finished here, I'll move that dresser back to Peter's room."

Chapter Nine

"*Denke* for going with me to see the pony," Sarah said as she and Rebecca pulled out onto the main road. "I hope he's nice. I'd love to surprise the kids."

The big gelding set off at a good clip, his hooves echoing on the pavement while the harness rings jingled, and white vapor puffed from his nostrils.

"*Nee* problem," Rebecca said. "It isn't even *that* cold today."

"*Gut* thing too since it's a long drive."

Rebecca glanced at Sarah and bit her lip.

"Okay," Sarah said. "I know that expression. What is it that you're debating telling me?"

Rebecca hesitated a moment then said, "Sarah, did you hear Thomas is already courting another girl?"

"What?" Sarah couldn't believe what she'd just heard. They'd barely broken up, and he'd already found someone else. It shouldn't bother her, but it did. Was she that easy to replace? Apparently so.

"I know," Rebecca said. "Your relationship has barely cooled before he chooses someone else. It's … disturbing."

It was, but there was nothing Sarah could do about it, so there was no point in dwelling over it. Regardless, there was no denying that it hurt to know she meant so little to him. Had it always been like that, and she just didn't know it? Had he been looking for a way out? Who knew, other than Thomas himself?

She was going to try to not let it bother her. It was just a failed relationship. And life was full of them. She was going to concentrate on the future and her role with the children. Nothing else mattered at the moment.

Thomas had proven that to her more than anything else could have. She had a feeling that Daniel would never have acted so crassly. He didn't come off as that sort of man, despite his earlier mistake.

But then, why should she be thinking of him in that way at all?

They drove through farmland with open fields on both sides of the road. The remains of corn stalks poked up here and there, but otherwise, the ground lay cold, waiting to awaken in the spring.

"How'd you hear about this pony?" Rebecca asked.

"Saw an ad for him on the board at the mercantile. He sounds perfect. Other than the price."

"Horses are going high right now," Rebecca said. "If you went to the auctions, you'd see what I mean. People are making so much money selling horses to the *Englisch*. Even ponies are going for *gut* money. That's why a *gut*, kid-safe pony will set you back."

"You know more about horses than a lot of our menfolk," Sarah said.

Rebecca snickered. "If I had my way, I'd be driving a flashy black and white pinto everywhere I went. But the bishop would frown on that sort of thing. I don't mind our plain clothes, but I would like a bit brighter colored horse."

"A black horse looks elegant," Sarah said.

"True, but bays are a dime a dozen. Seems like that's all we drive."

They reached town and passed through. The farm they were going to was on the other side of town.

"So are we going to discuss your new employee?" Rebecca asked and grinned.

"*Ach,* him. Why?" Sarah said.

"Come on, I want to know what he's like. I've heard he's quite handsome. Is he?"

"He's nice-looking, I suppose."

"You suppose, huh? That probably means he's as handsome as gossip says he is." Rebecca said.

Sarah laughed. "He's handsome. And he's highly skilled in his work. I feel fortunate that he answered my ad."

"I'm glad you found a *gut* worker."

"He's practically running things by himself already," Sarah said. "We've been talking about some ideas to expand the business. And that's about all I know about him."

"Interesting," Rebecca said. "Sounds like this man could be a real blessing."

"I'm glad I hired him," Sarah said.

"I guess so. How much further is the farm?"

"We should be getting close. They said it was near a water tower, and I see one just ahead."

Sarah drove the horse another mile until she saw a white fence that seemed to go forever. "I think we found it," Sarah said and turned into the drive when they eventually came to it.

The house was huge, and a scattering of barns dotted the property.

"My," Rebecca said. "Look at this place. This is amazing."

"Everything looks expensive," Sarah said.

"Including the ponies," Rebecca said dryly.

They stopped near a barn where a short, middle-aged Amish man pushed a wheelbarrow. He came over to the buggy. "Can I help you ladies?"

"I saw an ad posed for a silver dapple black pony for sale," Sarah said.

"I know the one you're talking about. I'm Robert Kemp, and I work here. I can show you the pony."

"*Denke*," Sarah replied.

"If you like him, we can harness him to a cart and you can try him," Kemp said.

"That would be fine," Sarah said.

"Come this way," Kemp said. "He's in this barn."

They followed the man into the barn, past spotless stalls that all perfectly matched with fancy hanging lights.

Kemp led them to a stall near the end where a silver dapple black pony with a lighter mane and tail stood munching hay.

"He's dappled when he sheds out all that hair," Kemp said. "He's ten years old, in his prime, and broke. This is the owner's daughter's pony. She outgrew him a couple years ago, and he's just been a driving pony ever since."

"Can you bring him out of the stall?" Sarah said.

"Certainly," Kemp said and went into the stall and led the pony out. He moved easily, walking when Kemp walked and stopping when Kemp stopped.

"If you'd like to try him with a cart I can harness him for you."

"*Jah*, please," Sarah said.

"Come to the arena, and you can drive him." Kemp led the pony to another barn housing a huge indoor arena. He harnessed the pony and hitched him to a small cart.

Kemp said, "Go ahead and try him out. You'll love him."

Sarah climbed in the cart and took the lines. She clucked, and the pony walked out. He stopped at the lightest touch. She took him to the left, then turned and drove to the right. She backed him up, turned him in a tight circle, and he behaved perfectly—just as he was advertised.

She took him around a few more times. She wanted him badly. The children would love him. He would make a wonderful Christmas present, but he was so expensive.

But she did have enough money from selling the cattle. And the woodshop was coming along. She bit her lip.

Rebecca watched from the side with a grin on her face as if she knew Sarah was struggling with the price.

The children had lost everything. What was more important? A trustworthy pony they could drive with confidence or a few extra dollars. Sarah pulled up and got out of the cart.

Kemp came over with a questioning look on his face.

"I'll take him," Sarah said.

Chapter Ten

"I'm sorry, Daniel. I just can't watch him any longer," Mrs. Weiss said. "I don't want to leave you in a bind. And I had *nee* idea I wouldn't be able to do this long term. But my *dochder* has begged me to move to Illinois before Christmas. I would watch Samuel from now on if I was staying. He's a *wunderbar* little boy. But with my son-in-law now disabled, my *dochder* desperately needs help."

"I understand," Daniel said, trying to hide his intense disappointment. "*Familye* has to come first."

Now what in the world was he going to do? It surely left him in a jam. He sympathized with her, but how could he work if he couldn't find someone to watch his son? He supposed he could take Samuel to work with him, if he couldn't find anyone. But he really didn't want to have to do that.

Samuel was a good little boy and would sit there all day if he was told to. But Daniel didn't want him doing that. He needed to have fun and be a child. He would have to sit and pay attention soon enough in school.

Samuel had been just a little too young to start school back in August. With his birthday falling in late November, he wouldn't begin classes until the following year.

Maybe Sarah would know of someone who could watch Samuel while he was at work. Over the last weeks, they had started becoming friends. He wasn't even sure how it had happened. But he now stopped at her house just about every night. And if she didn't need help with something around the house, they just had a cup of coffee and talked about the business. He fully supported what she was trying to do to support herself and the children.

~

Daniel was glad when the workday was over, and he was looking forward to a cup of hot coffee and some conversation. The men he worked with were mostly silent; neither of them was very good at carrying a conversation that went beyond what they were working on at the moment. He had explained some of the advancements he and Sarah wanted to make, and they had shown some interest.

Of course, they did the necessary work without complaint and did it well. But sometimes he just wanted to talk about things beyond a slab of wood. He didn't even bother to ask if either of them knew of someone who could watch his son. He knew they wouldn't.

Daniel went to the back door of Sarah's house and knocked lightly.

Sarah answered with a smile and ushered him inside. "I have the *kaffe* brewing."

"I can sure use a cup," he said and sank gratefully into the kitchen chair.

"Is something wrong?"

He let out a long breath. "The lady who watches my son is moving in a week, and I have *nee* one to take her place."

"I can watch him," Sarah said without hesitation.

"What? *Nee.* I can't have you do that."

She frowned. "Why not?"

"Well...I don't want to take advantage of your kindness, for one thing."

"Nonsense," she said. "I took care of Anna and Peter at that age. I can watch Samuel just as easily."

"Are you sure you wouldn't mind?" he asked, daring to hope.

"Why would I mind? I know he's a *gut* little boy."

"Well, I don't know. It feels like I'm imposing."

"You aren't," she said and rose to get the coffee.

He had to admit, the idea had a lot of appeal. Sarah was wonderful with her niece and nephew. She had a natural way with children.

"Are you positive you wouldn't mind?"

"Of course, or I wouldn't have offered." She poured their coffee and added cream and sugar to hers.

"Then I'll take you up on the offer." He let out a sigh, finally able to breathe easily now that his dilemma was solved. "He's a *gut* little boy. He won't be any trouble."

"I'm sure he won't," Sarah said.

He took a long drink of the hot coffee. "This *kaffe* suits perfectly."

She laughed. "I'm surprised you didn't just burn off your taste buds."

"It's best when it's hot."

"It's hot all right," she said. "Bring Samuel tomorrow, and I'll fix dinner for all of us. It'll be nice."

"Are you sure? That's a lot of work."

She laughed. "I'm already cooking for three. It's *nee* more work. Besides, I love to cook."

"Okay, then. That sounds right fine." He figured she would be a good cook. Already he was looking forward to supper.

~

The next morning, Daniel brought Samuel with him, and Sarah ushered them inside.

She squatted before the young lad. "Hi, Samuel. Remember me? I'm Sarah."

Samuel grinned and stuck close to Daniel. "Hi."

"You're going to spend the days here in my home. We'll have lots of fun."

He giggled. "Okay."

"I have a niece and a nephew who live here. They're getting ready for school. I walk them to school each day. Would you like to walk with us when they go to school?"

He nodded vigorously.

"*Gut.* We're going to have lots of fun."

"Well, it looks like you two will be okay," Daniel said. "I'll head to the woodshop."

"Everything will be fine here," she assured him.

Daniel nodded and left for the workshop.

Peter and Anna came from their rooms, eager to meet Samuel.

"Hi, I'm Peter."

"And I'm Anna."

"I'm Samuel," the boy said shyly.

"Get your coats and boots on," Sarah said. "We have to be going so you'll get to school on time."

Samuel stood and looked around while Anna and Peter got ready. When they had their outdoor gear on, they were ready to go. Samuel was still bundled in his coat and boots.

They left the house and set off for the road. Sarah took Samuel's hand.

She didn't have to worry about Peter and Anna getting near too near the lane of traffic, but she wasn't taking any chances with Samuel.

But she needn't worry, he stayed far away from the lines painted on the road, though they were barely noticeable beneath the packed snow and ice.

The three children laughed and giggled as they walked, and before they reached the school, they seemed like they'd been friends for a long time instead of less than an hour.

Samuel looked sad when Peter and Anna waved and ran to the school.

"I wish I was there, too," he said.

"You'll be starting next fall," Sarah told him. "It'll be here before you know it. You'll make more friends and learn all kinds of fun things."

He still looked sad.

"I have an idea," Sarah said.

He looked up at her. "What?"

"We could play school at home, if you want to." In this way, he could feel more included in learning along with Peter and Anna. And it wouldn't hurt to give him a leg up before he started school.

"*Jah!*"

"You want to do that?" she asked.

He nodded his head.

"Have you ever heard the Alphabet Song?"

He shook his head.

"What me to teach it to you?"

"*Jah.*" He bobbed his head with enthusiasm.

"Okay, I'll sing it, and then we can work on it together. Does that sound like fun?"

"*Jah.*" He grinned.

"Okay, here we go."

By the time they got back to the house, Samuel was singing the Alphabet Song with her and grinning from ear to ear.

She was impressed with his quick mind. She didn't know for sure yet, but maybe Daniel should have let him start school despite his late birthday. The boy was clearly very intelligent.

Sarah couldn't wait to teach him some further easy lessons.

"Do you know how to count to ten?" she said.

He nodded. He was such a charming little fellow.

"How high can you count?" she said.

"I can count to twenty," he announced.

She nodded. "*Gut.* We're going to have fun, and I'll teach you as much as you want to learn."

He clapped his hands.

"Is there anything special you would like for supper tonight? I'm going to make the meal for all of us?"

"Daddy, too?" he asked.

"*Jah.*" She smiled.

"Um, I don't know. I like everything."

"How about fried chicken?"

He cocked his head. "Do you know how to make chicken and dumplings?"

"I sure do. Would you like that?"

He nodded vigorously.

"Chicken and dumplings it is then," she said.

～

On the walk back to the school, Sarah and Samuel sang the Alphabet Song loudly. When they finished, they sang it again and again until Samuel could recite the entire alphabet. He clapped his hands and giggled at his achievement.

She smiled at him. "You've got it. You know the entire alphabet. Your *dat* will be so proud of you."

He clapped his hands again and giggled.

He sure was a happy little fellow. That spoke well of his father. Sarah was glad to know he treated Samuel so tenderly. For clearly, he did.

"Would you like to learn to count to thirty tomorrow?" she said.

"*Jah. Jah*," he said with infectious cheer. "Can you teach me to count to a hundred?"

"I can teach you to count as high as you like. But we'll just do a little at a time." She didn't want him to feel pressured when he wasn't even in school yet.

Peter and Anna raced out to greet them as soon as they reached the school.

"Let's get going," Sarah said. "I'm making chicken and dumplings tonight, and I need to get started as soon as we get home."

"Nice," Anna said. "I love chicken and dumplings."

"Me, too," said Samuel.

Sarah smiled to herself. She hoped Daniel liked chicken and dumplings, too.

~

Daniel was stuffed on the delicious meal Sarah had made. Not only was she beautiful, but she could also cook like a dream. And he couldn't believe it when Samuel proudly recited the alphabet perfectly, and then announced that Sarah had taught him how to sing it.

He was slightly ashamed that he hadn't thought of teaching Samuel the alphabet. But apparently Sam and Sarah had a great time singing the little song until he could sing it by himself and then recite the alphabet.

Sarah was amazing.

He'd learned through their conversations that the man she'd been courting had broken it off because of all her responsibilities. What a foolish man. How could he have thrown away such a wonderful woman?

Sarah was just a tad young, but she was very mature. She had found herself in a terrible situation, and she wasn't just making the best of it; she was helping everyone thrive. She would do well with the business. He knew she would. Although, he couldn't help but hope she would need a little guidance here and there.

Sarah had a lot going for her even if she didn't realize it. She was kind, generous, resilient, and smart. She was also lovely.

And he was quite sure she was unaware of just how much she had to offer.

He'd decided that if the bishop and elders tried to break up her little family, he would ask for the chance to speak up for her. Of course, it was no guarantee they would listen to him. But he would do his best for her. She was not an ordinary young woman.

Chapter Eleven

As the days ticked off and the deadline drew nearer, Sarah began to wonder if she really could do everything well. The pressure lay on her, weighing her down until she felt trapped beneath it.

She had no idea how the bishop and elders were going to see things. The woodshop was coming along well. But that was mostly thanks to Daniel. He might not realize it, but he was a complete blessing to her.

Though she did her best to hide it, Sarah was exhausted and emotionally drained. She took the best care she could of Anna and Peter and Samuel, when he was there. And she spent a lot of time every day teaching Samuel. He was a joy to work with, and his mind was amazingly quick.

But she couldn't stop worrying about the upcoming decision the bishop would render regarding the children.

She kept the house spotless and fresh despite the dirt and snow that were tracked in every time someone came in from the outside. She prepared the best meals she knew how to cook. And she made a large supper every night for them. Samuel and Daniel were now routinely joining them. In a strange way, they were functioning like a family. And all of them seemed happy with the arrangement.

It was the stress that was taking a toll on her. The unknown of what lay ahead ate at her constantly. And it grew worse with each day that took them closer to the Christmas deadline.

Sarah went to the kitchen to make some fresh coffee. Other than a bit of supper, she was mostly existing on coffee and water. She was too nervous to have much of an appetite, but she couldn't afford to come down sick again. Not now.

Every day, she made a good lunch for Samuel, but she didn't each much of anything herself. Instead, she relied on coffee to get her through the afternoon.

She put on the coffee pot and sat at the table for a few minutes while it brewed.

At least, the business was doing well—better than she'd hoped. They'd had a few new orders from her ad in the mercantile. And she'd contacted the owner of the website who did advertisements for Amish merchants.

She'd scheduled a meeting with him for after Christmas. She laid her head down on the table to rest for just a minute. Her eyes snapped open when Samuel tugged at her arm.

"That pot has steam pouring out."

"*Ach*," she cried and jumped up, snatching it off the burner.

"*Denke*, Samuel."

"You're welcome. Were ya sleepin'?"

"*Nee*. I was resting my eyes and didn't notice the steam." That was a fib. She had fallen asleep almost instantly. "I'm going to have some *kaffe*. Would you like to practice your counting?"

"*Jah*," he practically shouted.

She smiled at him. He loved learning. This child wasn't going to be a farmer. Not unless she missed her mark by a mile. He would surely be a businessman of some sort.

"Let me get a big cup of *kaffe*, and we'll do some counting," she said.

"Okay," he said with excitement in his voice.

~

The following morning, five days before Christmas, Sarah was up early. She had the coffee on, and she needed to get moving.

The kids weren't up yet, and Samuel would be arriving any time now. She needed to get everyone up and get breakfast on the stove.

She went to Anna's room and knocked on the door frame. "Time to wake up and get ready for school."

Anna cracked open her eyes. "I've been awake. I don't feel *gut, Aenti* Sarah."

Oh no. Now was not the time for anyone to get sick. If the child was sick, she had to miss school, which rightfully would not sit well with the bishop.

"Does your tummy or your head feel icky?" Sarah asked. She put her hand on Anna's forehead.

Anna trembled. "I'm hot and only my head hurts."

"You're burning up with fever," Sarah said.

Peter came in behind Sarah.

"What's wrong, Anna?"

"I don't feel *gut*." Anna didn't look well at all.

"Peter, I may need you to help me today, especially with little Samuel," Sarah said.

He nodded. "They're here. I saw them turning off the road."

"Go let Samuel in," Sarah said.

"Okay." Peter scampered off to let Sam in.

"I'll go make some chamomile tea to help with a headache," Anna said. "And I'll get a cool washcloth for your forehead." She heard the exhaustion in her voice.

"I'm sorry, *Aenti* Sarah," Anna said.

"There's nothing to be sorry for, honey. Just try to get comfortable and rest."

She hoped Anna wasn't coming down with the flu or something they would all catch. If both children got sick, that certainly wouldn't look good for the bishop. On the other hand, it wasn't like it would be because of something she had done wrong. No one wanted to be ill.

Honestly, she was letting her mind and her worry run away with her.

She heard Samuel's voice in the kitchen. She hoped he wouldn't pick up whatever Anna had. She wanted everyone healthy for the Christmas dinner she'd been planning for the last two weeks.

She went to the kitchen and made chamomile tea for Anna, and when it was ready, she filled a bowl with cold water and got a fresh washcloth.

She took the tea and the cold water back to Anna's room.

"Honey, let me prop you up so you can drink this tea.

Anna leaned forward so Sarah could put pillows behind her to lift her up.

Sarah gave her the cup of lukewarm tea, and then wrung out the washcloth. She placed the cloth on Anna's forehead.

"I'll be right back," Sarah said and went to check on both boys.

∾

Daniel hadn't even settled to work when Peter came out to the woodshop.

"Daniel, Anna is sick and *Aenti* Sarah's taking care of her today."

"What's wrong with your *schweschder*?" Daniel asked.

"Just sick, I guess," Peter said, shrugging.

"Okay," Daniel said. "We need to get you to school. If you're both home, it might not look *gut*."

Goodness, he was starting to worry as much as Sarah was.

"All right," Peter said. "Sarah wanted me to help her today, though. But if you think it's best, I'll go get ready."

"I'll go harness my horse while you're getting ready. We'll keep things going while Sarah's taking care of Anna. Don't worry about Samuel. He's my responsibility."

"Okay," Peter said and ran back to the house.

∾

Later that day, after Peter was home from school, Daniel, Samuel, and Peter took over the household work so Sarah could take care of Anna until she was well.

There wasn't much cleaning to do except mopping the kitchen floor where people came in and out all day. Daniel made it his responsibility to keep that area clean. The rest of the house was spotless as Sarah was meticulous at keeping house.

Daniel had known she was excellent at keeping things clean, but he hadn't really known exactly how good she was at it until he started looking for things to do and couldn't find any.

Dinner was another matter. Daniel knew she was excellent in the kitchen, too. But he wasn't. Still, he could cook enough to feed them. He was preparing chicken to fry when someone knocked on the door.

Samuel went to see who it was.

"Hello," Rebecca said with a confused look. "Where's Sarah?"

"Hi Rebecca," Peter said with a big grin. "Come on in. Anna's sick and *Aenti* Sarah is taking care of her."

The young woman stepped inside. "*Ach,* dear. Is Anna okay?"

"*Aenti* Sarah said she has a bug," Peter answered.

Rebecca nodded. She looked at Daniel.

He said, "I work in the woodshop. Sarah watches my son, and I'm trying to help her out."

She nodded, but her lips quirked up a little. "Would you like me to help with dinner? I'm quite able."

"I don't want to put you out," he said.

"Nonsense," Rebecca said. "I cook for my siblings all the time. I'll fry the chicken. And I'll make some soup for Anna."

Daniel let out a sigh of relief as she took over in the kitchen.

"I'll prepare enough food for a couple days," Rebecca said.

"I appreciate this more than you will ever know," Daniel said.

He could clean, do the barn chores, and get Peter to school. But he was never going to be great at cooking.

"I'll go take care of the animals with Peter while you're taking care of dinner," Daniel told her.

"Thank you," Rebecca said and began to hum as she got the chicken in the frying pan.

Daniel and Peter hurried out into the cold and went to the barn. They took care of the horses and mucked out their stalls. Then they fed the goats and chickens before heading back to the house. They let themselves into the warmth of the kitchen.

"I can watch the chicken if you want to go see Sarah," he said.

"That would be helpful," Rebecca said and hurried off to Anna's room.

Daniel let out a little sigh of relief and went to make sure the chicken wasn't sticking in the frying pan.

It dawned on him that he was enjoying taking care of Sarah's chores and helping her as much as he could. He would gladly do the same every day until Sarah was able to take over. No way was he going to let Peter miss going to school when it would surely get back to the bishop and the elders. That wouldn't be helpful at all.

Maybe Sarah did need a little help, but she was a good caregiver and homemaker. She loved Anna and Peter, and they were better off with her than with anyone else.

Sarah was a strong, resilient young woman, even if she didn't realize it. He had nothing but respect for her. And he liked her. A lot. In fact, he was certain that what he was feeling for her had the potential to bloom into something much more.

He'd only felt like that once before, and he'd married that young woman.

Samuel asked, "What d'ya want me to do?"

"I think we have it under control," Daniel said and ruffled Samuel's blonde hair. "Let's go back to the house."

Inside, Rebecca had returned to the kitchen and was rooting through the pantry. She selected some canned goods and found a big pan. "I'm going to make a big pot of soup. There will be enough for all of you to have some if you want."

"That's really kind of you, Rebecca."

She smiled. "Sarah's my best friend. I'd do anything to help her if she was in need."

"You're a *gut* friend," Daniel said.

She grinned. "Besides, she looks downright worn out. It sounds like you're a *gut* friend, too," she said and smiled.

Had Sarah said something nice about him? He wanted to think she had.

"If you have the kitchen under control," Daniel said, "I'll go see how Sarah and Anna are doing."

"Sure, go on. I'll take care of the cooking," Rebecca said.

Daniel went to Anna's room, where she was sound asleep.

"How is she?" he said quietly.

Sarah left her chair and stepped out of Anna's room. "She's still feverish. I've given her some natural medicines, but the fever hasn't broken yet. I'm keeping cool rags on her forehead and insisting that she keep sipping water when she's awake."

"Do you want me to get a doctor for her?" Daniel said.

"Let's see how she feels tomorrow. If she's worse, then *jah*. We'll need the doctor."

"You make a *gut* nurse," Daniel said, smiling at her warmly.

"I don't know about *gut*, but I s'pose I'll do."

"Has she slept most of the day?" he said.

"On and off. I was going to read some of her books to her, but she doesn't stay awake long enough for me to finish any of them."

"I hope she feels better tomorrow," Daniel said.

"So do I. and if she isn't better, we'll go to the doctor."

Daniel wanted to stay there with them, but it didn't seem appropriate. "I'd better get back to the kitchen."

She nodded. "I smell chicken and soup."

"Rebecca's apparently a *gut* cook," he said.

"She is."

"We'll bring you a plate when supper's ready," he said.

She smiled. "Thanks. I am hungry."

He smiled back at her then left for the kitchen. Rebecca turned the chicken pieces then stirred the pot of soup.

"Can I do anything to help?" Daniel said.

"*Nee*. I've got it," she said.

Samuel sat at the table drawing snowmen on scrap paper.

Sarah was a good woman. Daniel doubted Anna's mother could have taken much better care of the little girl. Sarah was becoming important to him. There was no doubt about it. And oddly enough, he welcomed it.

~

Sarah felt a flush of warmth. Daniel was a good man. And so handsome. But she knew looks weren't important, though she couldn't help but enjoy them. He didn't have to spend so much time there helping, but she found herself touched and grateful.

He'd done all her outside chores. Earlier she had smiled to herself when she realized he was looking for something to clean. And she was sure he would have cooked for them except Rebecca had come to the rescue.

Daniel was the right kind of man. She couldn't help but compare him to Thomas, and Thomas came up lacking. She supposed it wasn't fair of her to judge, but she couldn't help it.

Daniel was a man of his word. He was a God-fearing man who wanted to live right and be a good community member. The kind of man with whom a woman could build a life and raise a family. He'd already proven he was good with children.

Maybe she shouldn't be thinking of him like that, but she couldn't seem to stop herself. Nor did she want to.

Chapter Twelve

The next couple of days passed quickly. Anna was much improved, but she was worn out and spent most of the days in bed with Sarah reading to her and in general, comforting her. Sarah knew that Anna was likely more needy because she was still grieving her mother and father, so she was happy to devote the time with her.

Fortunately for Sarah, Daniel arrived each day and took Peter to school, then he checked on the workshop to make sure the other two workers were staying on schedule. He did the chores, warmed up food, and checked on her and Anna regularly. He'd then rush off to get some work in, taking Sam with him.

She didn't know if she would ever be able to repay him for all the kindness he'd shown them; he was a true godsend. She had thanked God many times over the last few days for Daniel and all he had done for them.

She was especially thankful that he had driven Peter to school and then gone to pick him up. She could only imagine how the bishop would have reacted to Peter missing more days of school due to someone else's illness.

She remained worried about the bishop's decision on Christmas. She would only be able to relax once the situation was resolved. She couldn't imagine losing Peter and Anna. Not now. Maybe she wasn't perfect, but who was? In Daniel, she now had someone else who cared about them and wanted to help them. That alone uplifted her and helped her feel confident to take on and manage the responsibilities that came with raising her niece and nephew while running a business.

～

Two days before Christmas, Sarah awoke to the sound of laughter in the kitchen. It was Daniel and the boys. She was sitting in a comfortable chair beside Anna's bed. Her niece slept peacefully beside her.

She felt Anna's forehead and it was cool to the touch.

"Thank you, *Gott*," she whispered. "She's doing so much better."

She left the bedroom and headed for the kitchen.

Daniel saw her and smiled. "How's Anna this morning?"

"She's resting peacefully. She's truly on the mend."

"I'm so glad," Daniel said.

She came to the table and sat beside him. "*Denke*, for everything. You were an absolute godsend to us. I don't know what I would have done without you."

"You would have been fine," he said. "You're a strong woman. I just wanted to help so you didn't have to manage it alone."

"I'm so glad you did," she said. She wanted to tell him she thought he was a wonderful person. The kind of man any woman would be lucky to marry. But she couldn't say those kinds of things—*ach*, that would be unheard of.

"I've been planning a Christmas dinner for all of us. You'll come, won't you?"

What if he said no? She bit her lip.

"I'd love to come for Christmas dinner. I'll even help you in the kitchen."

She grinned. "You aren't bad in the kitchen after all."

"And you're great in the kitchen," he said. "I could eat your cooking every day. So could Samuel. He loves it."

"He's such a sweet little man," Sarah said. "I'm right fond of him. Your little boy is going to do well in life."

"I'm glad I'm not the only one who thinks so," Daniel said.

"You definitely aren't the only one."

She glanced about and smiled at them. They felt like family. Her family.

~

Christmas arrived colder than usual with a fresh blanket of snow on the ground.

Sarah had knitted scarves, hats, and gloves for all of them much earlier in the season. Even though it made her sad, she'd decided to give the set she'd made for her brother to Daniel. And she'd managed to knit a small set for Sam while she had watched over Anna. Each set was a different color. She hoped they liked them. She'd made them with love, and she would give them with love.

The last of the food was finished by one o'clock, and she set the table and then served the food. It looked lovely and would taste even better.

Her heart warmed at the people who would be sharing it with her. There would be two beloved souls missing, but she prayed they were rejoicing with God in heaven.

She watched Daniel and Samuel from across the room. They were smiling and laughing.

"Come everyone," she called. "Let's eat together."

They gathered around the table. "Would you start the silent blessing?" she asked Daniel.

"It would be my pleasure," Daniel said.

⁓

After the meal, Sarah brought out her gifts.

"We have gifts, too," Daniel said. He went out to the woodshop and came back a few minutes later with gifts for them.

She gave out her knitted sets and Daniel said, "I love it."

"Me, too," Samuel said and tried his on.

Daniel gave Anna a pretty gold and teal journal and both boys received books. He gave Sarah a small cedar bookshelf he'd made.

"I have one more gift, and it's for the *kinner*. Samuel, too, if you don't mind. The gift is in the barn," Sarah said, for she had already arranged for the pony to be delivered early that afternoon.

Daniel grinned. "I don't mind if it's what I saw earlier when I put my horse in a stall."

"It is," she said.

"I thought that was what it was," he said.

"Is it a pony?" Anna cried with excitement in her voice.

"A pony?" Samuel said.

Peter looked between Sarah and Daniel.

"It's a beautiful cart pony, but you can ride him, too," Sarah said.

Anna squealed and ran for her boots and coat with Peter and Samuel right behind her.

~

They spent the rest of the day playing with the pony and then in the evening, they sang Christmas hymns and told stories of Christmases from the past. The evening passed so quickly Sarah couldn't believe it. And one by one, the children fell asleep on the davenport, and it was just her and Daniel awake.

"Daniel," she said, wanting to thank him again. "I want you to know how much I appreciate everything you've done for us."

"I feel the same about all you've done for us," he said, and a little smile tugged at the corners of his lips. "I've ... well, I've come to care about you a great deal."

Her heart raced. He caught her hand in his and said, "We haven't known each other that long, but I admire you so much. I've fallen for you, Sarah. I know this might be fast. If it's too fast, we can take things slowly, and I'll wait. But Sarah, could you—would you consider marrying me? We could be a family, the five of us."

Her breath caught and tears filled her eyes. She couldn't believe this was happening, but there was a peace, a sureness in her heart. "*Jah*, Daniel. I will marry you."

~

Two days later, with Daniel beside her, they waited for the bishop and the deacons to arrive to talk about the situation with the children. But this time, she was no longer worried.

When they arrived, she met them at the door and asked them to come inside. She showed them to the front room and offered them coffee and pie, though no one wanted any.

She stood in front of them and before any of them had a chance to speak, she said, "I have *gut* news I'd like to share with all of you." She glanced at Daniel, and he nodded his head with encouragement. "Daniel and I have decided to marry. Together, we'll care for my niece, nephew, and his son."

The men looked at each other and then broke into chatter over the unexpected development.

"Sarah, you're a bit young to marry," the bishop interjected, but he was smiling.

A few deacons murmured in agreement.

"This is true," Sarah said, feeling bolder and surer of herself than she'd ever been in her life. "But you must admit that I have been through quite a lot in my short life. More than most people my age—the kinds of events that most people never have to face."

They talked among themselves for a few minutes, then the bishop said, "In truth, we're relieved and gratified that your *familye* will remain together. And may I say I'm grateful you're to marry. But Sarah, you've done a *wonderbar* job on your own, too. I know how hard you've worked. We were going to allow you all to stay together, but now, this is even better."

She nodded with tears in her eyes. It was over. Things were set. Everyone was going to be all right—better than all right.

"*Denke*," she said and let out a sigh of relief. Her family's future was secure now. She was secure in a way she'd never been before. She glanced at Daniel, and her heart warmed at the love she saw in his eyes.

Their future stretched out before them, bright and warm, like the rising sun. She couldn't wait to tell Anna and Peter that they never needed to fear being taken away again. It was over and done. They would start planning the future and their life together.

Epilogue

Ten Months Later

"You look beautiful," Rebecca said as she inspected Sarah's dress.

"I can't believe my wedding day is already here," Sarah said. "It seems like we just met. And here we are, getting married."

"It's so romantic," Rebecca said. "He came into your life like a knight on a white horse. You know, like one of those *Englisch* fairy tales."

Sarah giggled, but it was the truth.

Daniel was the best thing that had ever happened to her. He

was the sun that had shown bright and cheery through the clouds of hardship.

"Look," Rebecca said. "I see the bishop. He must be getting ready."

A flutter of nervous excitement rushed through Sarah. Very soon now, she and Daniel would be married, and their life together would begin.

They had a huge wedding feast prepared. And the afternoon and evening would be filled with friends, singing, games, and relaxation. It was a day she wanted to cherish for the rest of her life.

Even though they didn't do elaborate weddings like the *Englischers*, it was the most extravagant thing she'd ever had to prepare for. She'd made her own dress, and she had organized and arranged everything, which in truth, had given her joy.

She glanced up, and the bishop caught her gaze. He smiled and motioned for her to come forward. It was time. They were ready.

Taking a deep breath, she looked at Rebecca. "It's time. I'm so happy but also a bit nervous."

Rebecca laughed. "*Nee,* you aren't. You're going to go marry the *mann* you love and live a *gut* life. It's your happy ever after. Like the stories."

Sarah nodded and smiled. "*Jah*. You're right. It is." She took another deep breath and smiled again. "All right, let's go. It's time for the next part of my story to begin."

As she walked forward, she saw Daniel, off to the side behind the bishop, waiting for her. Her heart raced and she blinked back happy tears. Peter and Anna and Sam were there, too, in their spots on the front row. They were grinning widely.

She grinned back at them. "Thank you, dear *Gott*," she whispered and kept walking.

The End

Continue Reading...

✦✦✦

Thank you for reading *Aenti Sarah's Christmas*. Are you wondering **what to read next?** Why not read *The Christmas Nativity?* **Here's a peek for you:**

"So, you're going back? You're leaving?"

Amos Graber smiled at Freddie, his co-worker, realizing he was going to miss him the most when he returned home. When he arrived in Lititz exactly a year ago, Freddie was one of the first people to welcome him. He had given Amos a place to stay and even introduced him to Dennis, their boss and the head contractor at their firm. It was through him that Amos got a home and a place to work in a new town.

"I am leaving," he answered, seated on the top rail of the fence that bordered their house. His legs swung lightly from side to side.

Freddie leaned on the fence. "We're like brothers now. I don't even know where I'd be if you hadn't come into my life when you did."

"*Ach,* come on. That ain't true," Amos said.

"It is," Freddie said, his voice steady. "I'm being completely honest. You've changed me in more ways than you know. Your way of life rubbed off on me. I stopped drinking, picked up the Bible for the first time in years, and I even catch myself talking like you sometimes. It's a big compliment. Life became, well, better after I met you."

"You mean that?"

"One hundred percent." Freddie nodded. "You made me sit up at work, too. I worked harder, made double what I made last year. You're a good man, Amos. You're stubborn, and sometimes you can be very overbearing, but you're good. Disciplined. I like that about you. You never waver in your beliefs. Even when the ladies won't leave you alone, you don't take the bait. That takes a lot of self-control."

"*Danke,*" Amos said, feeling emotional. "I needed to hear that."

"You're welcome," Freddie replied. "So, you really have to go?"

"*Jah,*" he answered. "I really do."

"It's confusing," Freddie said and crossed his arms. "From what I understand, your father doesn't even like you. He's never responded to any of your mail. In fact, no one responds to your letters. Now, I don't actually know what you did that made you leave in the first place, but are you sure you want to go back and face the music?"

Amos stared into space, feeling a strange weight settle in his heart. A year had passed since he had last spoken to his father, or anyone else from Lancaster County.

VISIT HERE To Read More!

https://www.ticahousepublishing.com/amish-miller.html

Thank you for Reading

✦❈✦

If you **love Amish Romance**, <u>**Visit Here:**</u>

https://amish.subscribemenow.com/

to find out about all <u>**New Hannah Miller Amish Romance Releases!**</u> **We will let you know as soon as they become available!**

If you enjoyed *Aenti Sarah's Christmas,* would you kindly take a couple minutes to leave a positive review on Amazon? It only takes a moment, and positive reviews truly make a difference. I would be so grateful! Thank you!

Turn the page to discover more Hannah Miller Amish Romances just for you!

More Amish Romance from Hannah Miller

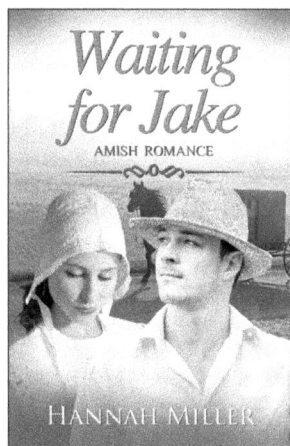

Visit HERE for Hannah Miller's Amish Romance

https://ticahousepublishing.com/amish-miller.html

About the Author

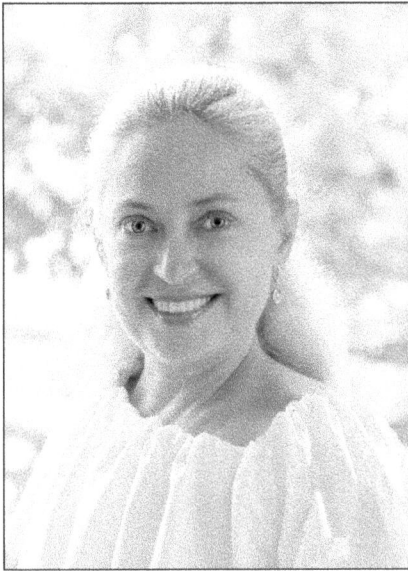

Hannah Miller has been writing Amish Romance for the past seven years. Long intrigued by the Amish way of life, Hannah has traveled the United States, visiting different Amish communities. She treasures her Amish friends and enjoys visiting with them. Hannah makes her home in Indiana, along with her husband, Robert. Together, they have three children and seven grandchildren. Hannah loves to ride bikes in the sunshine. And if it's warm enough for a picnic, you'll find her under the nearest tree!